WAR OF THE TRIBES

War of the Tribes
Written by Darius Cyrus Modi
Print Edition

First Published in India in 2021
Inkfeathers Publishing
New Delhi 110095

ISBN 978-93-90882-24-3

www.inkfeathers.com

WAR OF THE TRIBES

DARIUS CYRUS MODI

Inkfeathers Publishing

DISCLAIMER

The contents of this book are solely owned by the Author of this book and are in no way intended to hurt anyone's religious, political, spiritual, brand, personal or fanatic beliefs and/or faith, whatsoever.

Unless otherwise indicated, all the names, characters, objects, businesses, places, events, incidents- whether physical/nonphysical, real/unreal, tangible/ intangible in whatsoever description used in this book are either the product of the author's imagination or used in a fictitious manner. Any resemblance to actual persons, objects, characters, names, entities, living or dead, or actual events is purely coincidental.

In case, any sort of plagiarism is detected within this book or in case of any complaints or grievances or objections, the publisher shall not be held responsible whatsoever.

To my Grandfather

CONTENTS

PREFACE

Books have always been the script for their respective movies. The movies may not be the exact replica of the books, but if the books were best-sellers, the movies would generally be blockbusters. There are many famous movie series that had their origins in books.

Growing up reading fantasy books and watching movies, I felt that this was one genre where I could establish myself. With virtually no limits in this genre, writers can create their ideal world and immerse the readers into pages of whatever tickled their fancy. I am no different. I prefer non-linear storylines, preferably with plot twists and a sense of mystery. People say that the book cannot deliver the same feeling as the movie, but the books give you something that the movies do not. The fresh smell of the pages of a new book, the papercuts people sometimes get when turning the pages, the crisp print on the pages; these are things no movie can ever give you. I am not putting down any movies, but I do prefer books to movies. Books allow you to read lines and simultaneously imagine the scenes that are being played out, subject to an immediate change in your mind only. You can decide what soundtrack to play in your head while reading the lines.

If one has to ask the process that brought this book to life, I would say that it was one that started smoothly, with a couple of rough patches towards the end, but after sorting out those rough patches, it glided on to become the product you hold in your hands. The book started as a short story in January 2017. With some ideas thrown around by friends, I decided to increase the length of the story. From just 4 pages to a full book, it took me over a year, adding the final touches to the book in April 2018. It was not without hindrances. I had enough of distractions and mini writer's blocks. Whenever I would be in those situations, I would turn to my friends for some ideas. We used almost every resource at our disposal: computer simulations, stick figure action at the back of a classroom. There were times when I used concepts on myself, where applicable.

I always isolated myself when writing, so that I could keep it up for hours in the end. Music was my one constant companion through all this. I listened to a wide variety of music while writing.

Inspired by the work I did in this book, I started writing my second book in this series. I aimed to better the content, see how far I could push myself before even I would think my content was getting a bit out of hand, even for science fiction.

WAR OF THE TRIBES

CHAPTER 1

His first memories: a cold night, a woman singing, an urge to sleep. And then an orange flicker occurred and he was lifted up in strong arms. He heard a scream and then he fell unconscious.

Fourteen years later, he was sitting under an apple tree after a workout of two hours wondering whether he would like his instructor who was supposed to be coming from Adnanam, the town he stayed near to. The house was just outside the edge of the town, which gave him and his family some privacy. He heard his father call, "Ake, come and have your dinner." He sighed and got up. His family wasn't really related to him, but ever since they found him, under that very tree, as a little baby, they took it upon themselves to look after him. It was a seven-member family: his parents: Hadran and Sisha; sister Hasha, who was his age; his father's brother, who he had never met; his mother's sister, Fradki; and their Wolf, Hadver.

The family never made him feel uncomfortable and involved him all their activities. He excelled at Horse-riding and archery though he preferred a double-bladed axe as his weapon of choice.

As he headed to the house, Hadver ran to intercept him and jumped on him, licking him and didn't stop. Ake, laughing, pulled himself up and went inside the house. Inside, everyone was at the table, tucking into the food. He sat down and helped himself to some beef. The food was spicy, just as he liked it.

Half-way through the meal, Hasha sprung him a question, "Are you prepared for tomorrow?" Ake smiled and replied, "Yes, why?" Hasha said, "You have never looked so tense."

"Maybe," came the blunt reply. Turning to his father, he asked, "Have I ever seen this man?"

Hadran said, "No."

"What is his name?"

"He will tell you himself."

And with that, dinner was concluded.

As he was going to his room, Ake turned and asked his mother for a map of the land. It was given to him and he went to his room. Opening the map, he saw many symbols, most of which he knew. He saw their District, "Logder," the land of the Wolf fighters. It was so called because the people who lived in this region fought under the banner of a Wolf. Their armour was made of hard leather and the helmets were shaped like a Wolf's head. Their sacred colours were grey, blue and black. The gem sacred to them was an emerald. The sacred element was water. That meant that his family were Wolf citizens. There were other Districts, of course, the Districts of the Lions, Bulls, Ravens, and Horses. The Dragons, too, had a District, though not as advanced as the others. They were strong Districts with their own legends and legendary warriors and were formidable powers. Each had their own rulers and were united under one name, "Lasgalan," the land of the white gems. Looking at the map, Ake thought to himself, Will I ever visit these lands?

The ruler of Lasgalan was King Rendaf, a warrior of the Raven District and a man of prowess. His father whose name no one knew, had brought himself up from slavery and fought against the tyrant, Yedgal, and died after just one day on the throne. The first reform that Rendaf's father had introduced was the abolishment of slavery and because of his father, Rendaf was very popular.

Ake realised it was getting late and folded the map, climbed into bed and went to sleep.

Next morning, Ake was up at dawn. After lazing around in bed for another half-hour he got up, went down for breakfast and then went outside to be with Hadver.

Hadver was the only one in the family who listened to Ake, and actually obeyed him. He was a fast Wolf and could run one league in less than three minutes. His sharp fangs could rip a Lion open as if it were made of paper. Any stranger or thief coming into their plot of land would have to try and get past Hadver, which was impossible. If one saw Hadver in the dead of night, the only thing they would see were his green eyes and gleaming white teeth which could kill a Lion in one bite and crush bone in the same. His dark-grey muscular frame would make people think twice before trying to wrestle him to the ground as he weighed a little over 200 pounds and would only have to charge, jump onto them and they would be on the ground.

Hadver saw Ake coming and ran to him, barking away. For the next half-hour, they were running around the plot, Ake trying to outrun the Wolf. Hadran came to the door and watched them. He smiled as Hadver stopped, turned to bark at Ake, taunting him, before taking off again.

Later, when Ake was inside, he asked his father when his instructor was coming. A reply was given, "Within the hour."

Ake went outside and sat down on the front steps. Hadver came and put his head down on his lap. After a while, a hooded figure riding a Horse came up the path leading to the house. Hadver sprung up and let out a growl loud enough to be heard by the man and tensed his muscles, ready to charge the figure. Ake put his hand around his axe and gripped it tightly. He called out to the hooded figure, "State your business here, sir." With no reply or acknowledgement to Ake, the man got off the Horse and opened the gate calmly, without fear of Hadver. Hadver charged. With enough force to bring down a Bull, he jumped. The man stepped aside with ease and, with Hadver still in the air, brought his index finger down between his shoulder blades, incapacitating the huge Wolf. Hadver hit the ground and tried to get up, in vain. Ake could not believe his eyes. No one could have moved that fast. He was not liking the odds of fighting someone who could bring down Hadver with such ease. Nevertheless, he ran to the man, bringing down the axe with force that could fell a small pine tree. All of a sudden, he heard a clang of iron on iron and was shocked to see a sword in the man's hands. The man definitely could not have moved that fast. He pushed Ake backwards and the latter fell on the pathway. He got up and asked, "Who are you?" The man, pulling his hood back said, "I am your instructor for the next few months. Also, I am your uncle, Faldor."

CHAPTER 2

Ake stood stunned. Looking at Hadver he said, "What did you to him?"

"Oh, nothing. He will be alright." As if on cue, Hadver got up and started to lick Faldor's palm.

"Never underestimate Wolves." Faldor said. "They will be good to you as long as you are good to them. They have long memories so be careful of what you do to them." Hadran came out just then and Ake could see the similarities between the two brothers. Both of them were six and a half feet tall, had electric-blue eyes, short dark hair, and prominent jaw lines. The only difference was that Faldor's arms looked like they could crush boulders with little effort.

Hadran embraced his brother and asked him, "Do you want to meet the family, Faldor?"

"Sure."

Ake followed them into the house. The first person to see Faldor was Hasha, who nearly fainted at the sight of his arms. Sisha came out to meet him and started fussing over the state of his clothes, which looked nearly a week old. Fradki saw him and smiled shyly at him.

An hour later, Faldor was eating food. Ake was astonished at the amount of food he was ingesting. He looked at his uncle and without thinking asked him, "What is your weapon of choice?" Faldor looked at his nephew and answered, "A sword." He finished his food and told Ake, "Get your weapons out. We're starting your training."

Ake ran up to his room, fetched his axe and bow and arrows and ran to the back of the house, into the garden. There was a wooded area near it, so the family didn't have a shortage of wood when needed.

Faldor was sitting on the grass, watching him approach. He stood up and, in three giant steps crossed the width of the garden and started to duel Ake. There was no warning; he swung his sword straight at Ake's neck. Ake's instincts took over and he ducked, swinging his axe in the same motion at Faldor's knee, an almost fatal slice. With inhuman reflexes, Faldor jumped up, spun in mid-air, bringing his right leg out in a deadly arc, and kicked Ake in the chest. Ake flew back a good ten feet. He realised his uncle was a good fighter and the chances of him being beaten were low. Nevertheless, Ake got up and charged him. He swung his axe at his stomach, hoping to at least inflict a surface wound. Surprised by this move, Faldor hit him in his chest with the flat of the blade. Ake felt as if his ribs were being broken into small fragments. But he felt no pain for some reason. Out of desperation, he threw his axe at Faldor, cutting him on the shoulder. While he was distracted, Ake ploughed into him using his considerable bulk to his advantage and flattened his uncle. Faldor pushed him off and said, "That was the most unorthodox fighting I have ever seen. You are going to be a great fighter."

After eight hours of practice a day for the past month, Ake could see the visible change in his body. He was short and a little overweight; now he was tall and stocky. Hasha laughed at his difficulty in trying to slip on clothes.

One morning, when he was practising archery, Ake noticed his uncle was watching him. Faldor called him and took his bow and arrows and examined them carefully before saying, "Yew bow. Strong and yet quite flexible. Blackthorn arrows. You like to kill fast and painfully, without creating a noise. I like that in a warrior."

Later, when the family was eating lunch, Faldor asked Ake, "What do you know about the Legends?"

"What Legends?"

"You mean you don't know?"

"No."

"Faldor, he's too young. He doesn't need to know about them," Hadran spoke with a commanding voice.

But Ake had always been an inquisitive spirit. His interest got aroused and he turned to the brothers and said, "Too late. Tell me."

Faldor realised he had just walked into a trap that he himself had made. But there was no turning back now. He had to say everything.

"Ok. There are legends about every District of Lasgalan. The Wolves have dozens of legends, some of which will give you nightmares just by thinking about them. The first legend is that of Lord Logdan, the person who started the legendary Wolf Tribe and after whom our District is named. It is rumoured that his power came from an emerald ring that had the shape of a Wolf in gold stamped on it. It is said to be indestructible and that only a person of pure heart and from the Wolf District can wield it and harness the power of water and bend it to his or her will. The ring also commands every Wolf to defend the wearer of the ring to their last. Fire can't scorch it and dark magic can't influence it. It is that powerful."

"That would be a useful weapon to use in a battle." Hasha spoke up, breaking the silence that had fallen upon the table. Ake looked at his father and realised that he had never seen him look so angry. He glared at his brother so dangerously that Ake wondered if he was going to introduce Faldor's face to his mace though the former was unmindful of it. He continued, "Lord Logdan was said to have made a bow that had a body of elm, a Dragon-heart string and a drawn strength of five-hundred pounds. His quiver held a never-ending supply of birch arrows. It was considered virtually indestructible and was immune to influence of any magic."

"Faldor, that's enough!" Hadran commanded.

But Faldor needed to tell his nephew the secrets of Lasgalan, to prepare him for the future. So, he adamantly continued.

"The Sapphire Rose is a legendary flower that is blue and yellow in colour. It grows only on Bloodhound Mountain, some fifty leagues north of here. It can cure any disease, ailment or injury, no matter how grievous. Its juice is said to bring back people from the dead. Only a descendant of Lord Logdan himself can find the Rose. Only he can wear Lord Logdan's armour and wield his sword."

Ake was confused and it showed on his face. Faldor sighed and turning to Hadran asked, "What have you taught him? Does he know anything about the inheritance of the Wolves?" This apparently angered Hadran as he pushed the chair back gruffly, got up from the table and walked towards the garden. Fradki said, "I will handle him. He always listens to me." That was something no one understood; Hadran always listened to Fradki no matter how bad the situation was. She got up and followed him into the garden.

Faldor watched the retreating form of his brother, almost with contempt. Nevertheless, he turned back to Ake and continued, "Lord Logdan's armour was supposed to have been made of Dragon-hide. His sword was made of pure light and would pass through any person who it believed was being truthful. It was as if it had a mind of its own."

Hadran walked in, Fradki behind him. He looked at Faldor, grunted and walked to his room. Fradki said, "I've managed to calm him down for now, but now he doesn't want to talk to anyone." In all his life, Ake had never seen his father this angry. He looked at Faldor, who told Fradki, "He will calm down. Don't worry about him." Ake could swear that he saw his uncle wink at her.

After lunch, when Ake and Hadver were alone, Ake said, "I know this is stupid Hadver, but have you ever seen Dad get angry at Uncle?" Hadver looked at him with his intelligent green eyes as if to say "Maybe, maybe not." Ake sighed and got up. "I have to talk to him." Hadver suddenly jumped up and growled softly, in warning as if saying "No, you will not." Ake was a bit shocked by Hadver's actions. He had never acted like this before, at least not to Ake. Ake shrugged and tried to pass Hadver, but the Wolf growled a little more. Ake finally decided against seeing his father and went to practise his archery till supper. Hadran showed up for dinner, finished it in five minutes and without a word to anyone, went outside. Hadver finished his venison and proceeded to chew the bone until everyone had finished their dinner.

As Ake made his way his way to his room, Faldor stopped him and looking him straight in the eyes said, "Your father and I haven't seen eye to eye on everything, but he has to see that learning the Legends of Lasgalan is important, especially for you. Pray that he sees the light soon."

"But can't you just tell me why I need to learn them, Uncle?"

"It would take too much time to explain. But enough of talk. Get some sleep. You will need all your strength for tomorrow."

"Why?"

"Tomorrow, your real training begins."

CHAPTER 3

Early next morning, Ake woke up with Hadver licking his face. He shook the huge Wolf off himself and walked to the door. As he opened it, he saw his father at the bottom of the stairs looking right at him. Hadran spoke in a voice that barely concealed his anger. "Your uncle is in the garden. But first, I want you to see your sister. She wants to speak to you about something. Don't ask me what; I know not."

Ake went to his sister's room and saw her looking at him with a faraway look in her eyes.

"Please close the door, brother. I have to tell you something but I don't want anyone to know."

"What is it? You can trust me with any secret."

"You know Garon, the lad from next door?"

"Yes, why?"

Garon was a boy who lived on the opposite side of the woods at the back of their house. He was also a Wolf citizen, fifteen years old and used a dagger as his preferred weapon. His Wolf's name was Edmund. He was one of the few Wolves who stood a chance against Hadver in a fight or race. He was like Ake in many ways, with dark eyes, blonde hair and spoke few words. Though he (Garon) looked frail aside from his broad back, he could wrestle anyone to the ground in minutes.

"Well, I maybe in love with him."

"What!?" Ake was shocked.

Hasha smiled, blushing. "It is the truth. I don't know if he loves me though."

"So, it's just a crush then." Her brother looked as if some burden had been lifted from his shoulders.

"Yes, I've had it for the last few months. Please don't tell anyone."

"Ok. But you will tell our family yourself."

"In my own time."

Ake made his way to the garden. When he saw it, he realised that, probably overnight, Faldor had transformed it into a training block. Sandbags, archery targets, bows of different sizes and woods, arrows in their quivers hung neatly on racks, swords, spears and javelins in the same fashion. It looked as if Ake had walked right into a military training ground. Faldor pointed his sword at Ake's chest, "I will make a warrior of you, young man. In battle, you will be given no quarter, so for the next three months, I will teach you how to defend yourself in it."

Ake's first task was to string all the bows. The first wood was pine, a tree that he was familiar with. He picked up the first bow, which came up to his hips. He strung it easily. He moved onto the next size, which was up to his ribcage. This proved a bit difficult but he did it. The next bow came up to his shoulder which he strained his muscles trying to string. The last bow was as tall as him. He put one limb in the ground and tried to string it. It took him ten attempts and nearly twenty minutes. He finished with the pine bows and collapsed; his arms having got quite a workout. Faldor commanded, "No rest. Finish the rest of the bows and you get a break of a half-hour."

Ake looked at the bows left: yew, blackthorn, elm and birch. It took him another two hours to string them, blackthorn being the toughest. He finished them and reached for a glass and heard Faldor telling him that he had a half-hour to relax. His next task was to fire arrows at the targets. Nocking the arrows was easy. Pulling the string back to fire.... not so much. The strings were too tight and he nearly fainted trying to fire an arrow from the yew bow, supposedly the easiest bow from which to fire an arrow. His own bow was easy to fire from, but Faldor refused his using it.

The archery had many levels. He was learning how to shoot when the enemy was at the edge of his vision, without turning his head. By lunchtime, his arms felt as if they had been carrying rocks all day long, with neither food nor rest.

He trudged into the house, sweaty from his five-hour ordeal. Hasha took one look at him and collapsed into a fit of giggles. When she got a hold of herself, she said, "Sorry. I didn't mean to laugh. It's just that you look.... never mind, see for yourself." She held up a mirror, and Ake looked at his reflection. His shirt was ripped as if someone had cut through it with a sword. His arms had red lines all over them, the result of the string lashing out when he was stringing the elm bows. His blonde hair had fallen in front of his eyes like a curtain. His obsidian dark eyes looked like a ghoul's through his hair. His pants were ripped at the knees from when he had tried to string the tallest birch and blackthorn bows.

"I look like death." Ake reasoned.

"Not just that," Faldor said "You need more arm strength if you want to have any hope of winning competitive archery."

"Never, Faldor. My son is not going to go to Shodor for the Games. That is final." Hadran's voice rang loud and clear.

"He is, whether you like it or not."

When they were eating lunch, Faldor told his brother, "Your son has no arm strength. Would you care to explain this?" He spoke formally, like a person from the King's court. Ake wondered what lay in store for him for the rest of the day, forget the next three months. He could barely hold the spoon in his hand. He thought of the swords, spears and javelins that lay on their racks and just the thought of lifting them made his arms hurt. He finished his food and went up to his room. Hasha walked in behind. She sat on the edge of his bed and asked him, "Did you tell anyone?"

"No." Ake replied as he was still was trying to digest the fact that his sister had a crush.

"But why the sudden feelings for him? Surely there must be some reason for it."

She smiled shyly. Like always, Ake's question was well-aimed and to the point. Just then Faldor called out to Ake to remind him that he had five minutes of rest left.

Ake smiled and turned to his sister. "Don't worry. Your secret is safe with me." Just as they left the room, he gave his sister a peck on the cheek. Hasha blushed as red as a strawberry. The last time Ake did that, she had just turned eleven and he was still ten. Ake turned to face her at the bottom of the stairs. His once lost mischievous smile returned to his face. He last wore that smile two years ago, when he sprinkled extra pepper in her food and got her sneezing for over an hour.

"What? I am your brother. I'm pretty sure I can kiss my sister."

Hasha laughed and said, "Very funny, little brother. Now go on. You don't want to make Faldor wait."

When Ake set foot into the garden, he was astonished by how Faldor had cleared it. Everything was in one side of the garden. He wondered how his uncle had managed to do this in less than a half-hour. Faldor stood across the garden, Hadver next to him. Faldor said, "You have taxed your arms enough. So now let us see how fast you can run."

Ake wondered what his uncle was talking about. Nevertheless, he walked up to him and awaited the next command. But it did not come. Instead, Faldor bent and whispered something in Hadver's ear. The Wolf looked at Ake and, without warning, took off running. Ake understood what he had to do. He took off after the Wolf, who was not even going at half his usual speed. At the other side of the garden, a hundred metres away, a piece of venison was kept. Ake had to outrun Hadver before they reached it and Ake was not a bad runner. At the half-way point, when they were neck and neck, the Wolf let loose. Ake's leg muscles screamed as he tried to catch up with Hadver. By the time, he reached the three-quarter point, Hadver reached the meat and was chewing on it contentedly. Ake looked back at his uncle, who was watching. Faldor shouted, "Again." Ake walked back to the starting point and Hadver came as well.

"You just ran the length of the garden. Now you will do two laps of the perimeter."

Ake's legs nearly gave out. One length of the garden was a hundred metres. That meant he had to run about a little less than four hundred and fifty metres. It was doable in his own pace, but if he had to run against Hadver, who loved long-distance running, he was doomed. But if this was going to be helpful in the future, he figured it was important that he do it. Faldor shouted "Go," and they ran. Coming round the first of the eight corners of the garden, Ake was feeling confident.

Hadver seemed to be slowing down. This gave Ake a confidence boost. He sped up a bit at the second turn and lost Hadver in his peripheral vision. Then he made a dreadful mistake. Between turns two and three, he sped up, almost reaching full speed. At turn three, his speed began to wane and Hadver came back into his peripheral vision. Ake tried to speed up again but his legs refused to co-operate. He pushed his legs harder and saw Hadver, slowly coming in line with him with the same slow speed with which he started. At turn four, just before one lap was over, Hadver increased his speed slightly. Ake refused to give up and tried to pump his legs faster. At the one-lap point, Hadver clearly had enough. He looked at Ake in a taunting manner, as if saying, "Catch me if you can," and in less than ten seconds, reached his maximum speed. Ake had not even finished a quarter of the second lap when Hadver finished the race. He took a small lap round the garden and went to Faldor, who tossed him some meat.

"Hadver is too fast for me to outrun." Ake told Faldor.

"No. You're just too slow and a bit foolish. Honestly, who speeds at the sixty to seventy metre mark in a four hundred metre race? And it was not four hundred, but four hundred and fifty metres that you had to run," Faldor said.

"But why do I need to race Hadver? He is a Wolf, an animal that can easily outrun a human."

"You don't have to equal his speed; you just have to improve your speed and increase your stamina levels." Faldor said with a voice that signalled the discussion was over. From then till dinnertime, Faldor made Ake do sprints, Hadver behind him. Every time Ake slowed down, Hadver growled, encouraging him to run faster. Ake collapsed as soon as training was over.

"Why do my legs feel so heavy?"

"Oh, nothing really. It's just that without water or rest, lactic acid has built up in your muscles," Faldor casually tossed the comment, as if it was normal. He knelt next to Ake and putting his fingers behind his knees said, "Don't scream," and pushed his fingers hard, Ake's reflexes making him bring his calves almost up to his thighs.

"That's better. You can walk in about two minutes."

Ake went inside for dinner. Hadran took one look at him and told him to wash up and change his clothes. Ake was back at the table in fifteen minutes. As he tucked into his food, Faldor told him, "I am training you. I have taken months out just to come here, so don't make me feel like I am wasting my time."

"Brother, don't make him feel as if you are doing him a favour."

"Oh, I'm sorry. When were you planning on training him? When it was too late?" Faldor said angrily, in a sarcastic manner.

Hadran growled in a tone that was almost inhuman. He jabbed a finger at his brother and said, "I never should have asked you to come!"

"Then why did you?" Faldor countered.

Hadran got up and challenged him, "You and me. A duel. Now." Faldor calmly finished his dinner and got up. "If I win, I train him and take him to Shodor. If you win, I still train him but he won't go to Shodor."

"Fine," Hadran spat. They went to the garden, where there were still some rays of light, Hadran with his mace, Faldor with his sword. They stood twenty feet apart and with no warning to the other, charged. Faldor brought his sword down to his brother's waist, but Hadran saw it coming and used his mace to knock the sword out of Faldor's hands and his mace flew out of his hands in the same motion. Both the brothers were both without weapons and circled each other, in a wrestling style.

Just then, Hadver growled softly, as if he smelled something was not right in the air. Ake glanced towards the woods and thought he saw someone standing just behind the tree line. He was dressed in dark robes but his face was visible. He had dark hair, a chiselled face and held a sheathed sword in his hand. He seemed to be looking straight at Ake. Ake was about to draw the others' attention to him but Hasha beat him to it. She called out to the duelling brothers, "There's someone in the woods, looking right at us." The brothers stopped and looked straight at the man.

The figure realised his game was up, turned and ran into the woods.

CHAPTER 4

Ake had seen his father react to a situation fast, but not the way he and Faldor reacted just then. They got off each other, jumped the garden fence and ran towards the woods, Ake and Hadver right at their heels. Just as they neared the woods, they heard a crash and ran to where they thought the sound came from. Hadran was a good tracker but was surprised to see that no footprints were left by the man. Ake had not seen his father being fooled before when tracking something. He realised that even Hadver couldn't get a scent. Then they heard someone curse and saw a few birds flying up from the trees. They ran straight ahead and, in a few seconds, saw the cloaked figure running in front of them. He was fast, granted, but Hadver was faster. He tore ahead of the group at lightning speed, closing in on the figure quickly. He lunged at him, but the man seemed to sense the Wolf's movements. Without turning back, he lashed out the sheathed sword, knocking Hadver on the snout. Hadver fell to the ground, but almost instantly got up and gave chase again.

Ake had been in the woods many times and thought he knew it properly. But the figure seemed to be taking them deeper into the woods. Daylight was fading, but they could see the figure clearly. At that moment, when they felt they couldn't give chase anymore, they heard a howl and saw movement on the left. A Wolf with a reddish-maroon coat shot past them. Ake felt elated. He knew this Wolf. Help was not far away. As if on cue, a figure charged out from behind a bush, a dagger in each hand.

Flinging one dagger, he shouted, "Get him, Edmund!" Ake had never felt happier to see a dagger-throwing boy in his life. Together, the four males chased the figure through the woods, their Wolves closing in on him fast. Ake tried to catch up with the Wolves, but the terrain was working against him. Fallen trees and branches, huge rocks, all seemed to be slowing them down, but not the man or the Wolves. Hadver was literally nipping at the man's heels, Edmund just behind him. Just then, a gust of wind occurred and lifted the man's robes for a second before dying out. Ake looked at him, stunned. He turned to face Garon, who nodded at him, indicating that he also saw the suit of armour under the stranger's robe. They appeared to be approaching a clearing, as they could see it through the trees. The man seemed to be heading straight to it.

Suddenly, the brothers broke off from their group, running in opposite directions, skirting the clearing. Ake understood what they were planning to do. He and Garon gave each other some room and continued to pursue the figure. They managed to head the man into the clearing at the same time Hadran and Faldor emerged ahead of them, at the opposite side of the clearing. Hadver and Edmund pulled back, having successfully chased the man into the clearing.

The man realised that he was trapped, though his face betrayed no emotion. The two brothers were in front of him, the Wolves, just on the edge of his peripheral vision and the two boys behind him. The older boy had a dagger in his hand. The men themselves had no weapons, though one man's arms made up for the loss. The other one looked ready to take him on without weapons. He turned around carefully, careful not to make any sudden movements. The younger boy looked like a trained runner, though he must have been having other abilities. The man prayed in his heart, "Please let them be the ones of the Prophecy. Please, please." He needed to get out of there fast or else the Wolves would attack. He threw away his robe, revealing his suit of armour underneath. Ake could not see what was on it, but his uncle and father evidently recognised the armour. They closed in on the man fast. The man raised his arms up and chanted something, an incantation, most likely, and Ake saw that he had some orange tattoos on his arms. Suddenly, the air pressure dropped so rapidly that Ake's ears popped and a strong wind buffeted him. Judging by the way everyone was thrown backwards, it was obvious that the man had summoned the wind and it was coming away from him at high speed. The sudden drop of air pressure was enough to knock Ake unconscious. When he got up, he was still in the clearing. The sun had set at least an hour ago. As soon as the others got up, they walked back to the house. On the way, Ake asked Garon, "What were you doing in the woods?"

"That man had been watching my house for the past week. When he didn't show up today, I felt a little confident and took Edmund with me to hunt some rabbits for dinner tonight. Then at one point, he growled softly, like he did when he smelt that man. I crouched behind a bush and in a minute, he shot past us, chased by you guys. And well, you know the rest."

"How fast can Edmund run? Last I saw, he ran a league in just under five minutes."

"Now it's one league in three and a half minutes. By the way, who is that man," Garon pointed his chin towards Faldor, whose back was to them.

"My uncle, Faldor. I met him last month when he first came to our house."

"I would not want to try and fight him. He'd finish me in about two minutes."

"He took out Hadver in about five seconds."

"Forget it. I have no intention of fighting him," Garon said, laughing as he playfully pushed Ake on the shoulder.

They reached Ake's house, where Hadran and Faldor went straight up to Hadran's room, after briefing the women about what chanced in their encounter, and closed the door. Sisha told Garon that he could stay at their house for the night; she would send a message via pigeon to tell his parents that he was with them. Edmund and Hadver hungrily lapped up water and chowed down on venison. Hasha sat across the table from Garon, trying to make eye contact with him. Fradki popped a question to the two boys, "What happened out there?"

"Honestly, I don't know," Garon said "The man seemed to know exactly where he wanted to be. I think that the clearing worked to his advantage." He looked at Ake for support.

"Garon's right," said Ake. "That man summoned winds from nowhere. He wore a suit of armour with some designs on it. I don't know what they were, but I think dad and uncle recognised them. His robe which he had taken off was not there either. So, we have no way of tracking him."

"But did he say anything?"

"He said something that conjured up the wind. I couldn't catch the words, but it wasn't in a language I knew."

"He had some orange tattoos on his arms," Garon reminded him.

"What kind of tattoos?" Hasha asked him.

"No idea. It looked like a snake's head." Garon replied.

Ake wondered how he had seen that at the distance they were standing from the mystery man. Nevertheless, he kept quiet. He suddenly asked, "How can we be sure that it was a man we were chasing? He ran a little faster than Hadver and Edmund. Also, only he and the Wolves weren't fazed by the terrain. They ran on it with ease."

"Wait a minute, Ake," Garon said. "Are you suggesting we were chasing an animal who was made into a man by witchcraft?"

"No. I am just saying that maybe he was a man, with maybe the brain, muscles and instincts of an animal."

"That's impossible. No one can live like that," Fradki said, almost like she was trying to convince herself of it.

"All right boys, you can go to bed now," said Sisha, entering the room. "Garon, your parents have replied saying that you can stay the night and can go back tomorrow after breakfast. Both of you can sleep in Ake's room, there's space for all three of you; Hasha, you are included."

The boys ran up to Ake's room, skipping two steps at a time, Hasha coming behind them. Ake pulled out three rugs to sleep on, but Garon said, "Who sleeps at this hour of the night? Let's talk for some time."

They sat down on their own rugs and Hasha asked Garon, "What made you take a dagger as your weapon of choice?"

"I always had a fascination for small, sharp things. So, I chose the dagger. Also, in combat, a swordsman can't use his sword because I would be well inside his sword reach."

Ake asked Garon, "What weapon does your father use?"

"He likes archery. He can hit a target a hundred feet away." Garon replied.

"Garon," Hasha asked "Why does Edmund have a red coat? When he was small, he had a grey coat."

"Actually, about three years ago, he was chasing a rabbit through the woods when he tripped on a stone and tumbled on the red coloured soil there. We tried getting the colour off his coat, but it stuck. Within a week, the colour spread all over the original coat and he is now like this."

Something in Ake's mind clicked, but it seemed too much of a coincidence. But he said it. "Hasha, even Hadver's coat was never a dark-grey. It used to be a black colour."

Realisation dawned on Hasha's face. "You don't think that they're connected, do you," she asked Ake.

"I don't know."

Just then, Hadver and Edmund walked in. As Ake shut the door, he saw Hadran and Faldor talking in hushed tones to Sisha and Fradki. Hadran's vein was showing on his forehead, as it normally did when he was agitated or worried. Ake shut the door and facing the four of them said, "I don't know what's going on, but dad is very worried. His vein is showing." He glanced at Hadver, whose head was on Hasha's lap, and then to Edmund who was getting his back scratched by Garon. Why had he not noticed it before? Hadver and Edmund may have had different coats, but their physical structure was the same: same snout length; same growl and they had the same shade of green in their eyes, which was impossible. No two Wolves had the same shade of colour in their eyes. There was always a variation. But Hadver and Edmund had the exact same shade of green in their eyes. It was like they were copies of each other.

Suddenly, Edmund growled softly and moved close to the window. Ake moved swiftly to it and looked outside but saw no one outside. Suddenly, he was thankful of the Wolves being in the room. They would smell someone before he made it inside the house. After an hour of talking, they went to sleep.

What they did not know was that, when Edmund had growled, there was a man standing in the garden. Before Ake came to the window, he had jumped onto the roof and crouched on it, careful to not make a sound. Thankfully, the Wolves did not smell him. Once he was sure that they had all gone to sleep, he jumped down to the garden, rolling as he hit the ground so that there was hardly any sound produced by the impact. He walked to the edge of the garden before turning to face Ake's window and say, "You will help us, prophesied ones. You will correct everything that is wrong in this world." So saying, he climbed over the garden fence and walked into the woods.

CHAPTER 5

The next morning, the three of them woke up at dawn with the Wolves and watched the sun come up over the woods. Hadran and Faldor came in an hour later to call them to breakfast. When they were eating, Edmund and Hadver ran around the garden chasing each other. Garon asked Hadran if he could leave for his house after breakfast; his parents had asked him to. Hadran said, "Only with me accompanying you." After breakfast, while Hadran was escorting Garon to his house, Ake went to the garden and studied the swords. They were of different sizes, but the one thing common to them all was that they had a hilt with a Wolf's face on it.

Ake heard his uncle come into the garden, and waited for a command. It came: "Pick up a spear, lad." Ake picked up one from the rack and struggled to keep it up. Then Faldor told him to throw it at a sandbag, twenty metres away. Ake ran a short distance and threw the spear. It sailed through the air and fell on the ground ten metres from where Ake had released it.

"Pitiful, pitiful. How can you hope to kill anyone in combat if you throw like that?"

"It's too heavy to lift."

"Please. It's all in the way you hold it." Faldor walked to the fallen spear, put his feet under it and lifted it up, catching it as it came up. He took two steps and threw it. It pierced the sandbag and flew through it, landing about ten feet away from the bag. "That should be the way your spear is thrown, so that it can be reused. Try it again"

Ake lifted another spear and taking a short run, threw it. It landed two feet away from the sandbag. Not bad, he thought to himself. It's an improvement.

"Again." Faldor called.

Ake picked up another spear which had a blackthorn shaft. It felt surprisingly light and just right in his hands. He didn't take a run; he threw it from his place. It went through the sandbag without dropping in its flight and landed point-first in the ground. Ake looked at Faldor, whose face didn't conceal his shock. He looked at Ake, as if wondering how he had thrown it without a run. Nevertheless, he regained his composure and said, "Again." So, for the next three hours, Faldor made Ake throw spears at sandbags at different distances, ranging from ten metres to fifty metres. Almost all the spears went in.

Hadran came to the garden at one point and asked Faldor to come inside for a few minutes. Faldor asked Ake to keep practising. But Ake was determined to find out what his father was telling Faldor. His vein was still showing, so Ake was sure that Hadran was worried. He picked up a spear and threw it at the sandbag, missing it. It stopped near the brothers. He went to pick it up and heard Hadran saying, "Even Garon's parents said that they found it with him. Ake and he have to be from the same place as they said that Garon is not their own son."

Ake decided that he would pay a visit to Garon during his half-hour break after lunch. Faldor came back and told Ake that he had a break till after lunch, from when they would start practising with swords. Ake saw his opportunity. He went into the house and went straight to Hasha's room. She was looking out of the window and didn't hear him come in.

"Hey, sis," Ake said. She turned in surprise. "I'm going to Garon's house. Hadver is going with me."

"Ok. But why are you telling me?"

"Just so that you don't need to worry about me being missing." Ake said with a twinkle in his eye.

"Oh, very funny, brother. Now go."

And with that, Ake was out of the house running towards the woods, Hadver alongside him. They plunged into the woods and walked to Garon's house, a ten-minute walk. When they were a minute away from exiting the woods, Ake saw a Horse tied to a tree. Its coat was so dark that it would have camouflaged itself inside the woods. Anyone looking from Garon's house wouldn't have seen it, even if they were looking right at it. Ake thought about looking for the rider but decided against it. Just then, Hadver growled so softly that Ake thought he was going to jump the Horse, the latter not having seen them. Ake saw a man ahead of them, peering into Garon's house from behind a mulberry bush. Somehow, he sensed their presence. He turned slowly to face them. Ake realised, with icy certainty, that it was the same man from the day before. The man spoke first, "Have you come to accept your destiny, young one?"

"I've come to see what you've being doing." Ake bluffed, hoping to catch the man off his guard. "So, start talking." However, Hadver didn't want the man to start talking; he leapt at him, going straight for the head. The man seemed to know what he was going to do and bent backwards from his hips, causing Hadver to shoot over him, the bush and land behind the bush. Hadver howled so loudly that Ake was sure his father and uncle would have heard it. Suddenly, another howl responded and a red figure shot over the fence of the house. The man saw that he could not stand and fight, so he ran to the Horse. Ake had barely moved as he saw the man jump on the Horse. Not even Faldor could have jumped those two metres without a run. Out of nowhere, a dagger shot past Ake's ear and impaled itself on a tree behind the Horse, drawing a little blood from the equine. The Horse didn't need any coaxing to burst into a gallop. It shot into the woods before the Wolves could react. Ake turned and saw Garon running to him. He yanked the dagger out of the tree and turning to Ake asked him, "Was that the same chap from yesterday?" Ake nodded. Garon held the blood-stained dagger to the Wolves, allowing them to smell it. They immediately started snarling, indicating they were ready to track the man. "Ake, let's go." Garon's voice brought him to reality. He had now started to understand why his sister had fallen for Garon. The Wolves turned to see if their masters were ready, and ran into the woods. Ake and Garon saw drops of blood on the ground and ran harder. The Wolves suddenly stopped and growled, looking ahead with bared teeth. Garon advanced, dagger in hand. They saw a log in front and heard heavy breathing behind it. Edmund peered over the log and barked, as if in challenge. The boys saw the man sitting on the ground, the Horses head on his lap. He spoke to the Horse calmly and the equine slowly closed his eyes. The man then spoke, ceremoniously, "You sustained my body at times when I was weak. But now, with your death, you shall sustain me forever."

At the last word, the Horse dissolved into orange lights which went around the man and shot into him. A small gem, which Ake didn't recognise was left behind on the ground. The man picked it up and kept inside his robes. He got up and faced them. Between Garon's daggers, Ake's considerably muscled arms, which were due to using his axe to fell trees, and the two Wolves' teeth, the man did not stand a chance. But he held his ground and slowly brought his sheathed sword out from inside his robes. He removed the sword, a one metre long piece of double-edged silver. Ake instantly recognised the silver as Sisha, his mother, kept a piece of it. "To keep away the evil spirits," she used to say. He pointed the sword at Garon and flicked it to the side. Even though they were more than ten feet away, Garon's daggers flew out of his grasp and landed on the ground near the man. Garon looked at his daggers, dumbstruck. Never had he been disarmed so easily, that too with no contact with his foe. The man looked at the two Wolves who were growling and baring their teeth at him. He made a growl deep within his throat and the Wolves backed up three feet, still growling. He turned to the boys and said, "Accept your destiny, young men, before it is too late."

Ake had no idea what he was talking about. He looked at the man's arms, and realised Garon was right; there was an orange tattoo of a serpent-like creature on his arms. Before he could say anything, he heard something being thrown and instinctively ducked. A sword flew past him and narrowly missed the mystery man, hitting a tree and ricocheting off it back into the thrower's hand. Ake turned to see Faldor running towards them, with a man behind him who Ake took to be Garon's dad, as he had a bow and an arrow nocked in it. Faldor had Ake's axe in his hand.

The man turned and ran away from there, but clearly Faldor was not going to let him get away. He threw Ake's axe to him as he passed him and all four of them plunged deeper into the woods after the man. Hadver and Edmund chased the man at full speed but had a tough time trying to catch up to him as he had a significant head-start on them. While they were running, Ake told Faldor how the man could run the way he did and the gem that formed when the Horse dissolved. Faldor stared at the man's back and cursed. "How could I have been so foolish? Did he tell you anything else?"

"Yeah. He said something about us accepting our destiny before it was too late or something."

Faldor looked as if someone had slapped him across the face and muttered to himself, "We have to find the third one fast."

Before Ake could figure out what his uncle meant by that, the man stopped and pointed his sword at Faldor and shouted, "You better find the third one fast before she falls into the enemy's hands. I charge you to do this."

"Under what compulsion must I do it?" Faldor tried to show bravado as he spoke.

"I am a Talon, and so you must."

CHAPTER 6

Faldor stood rooted to his spot. He knew of the legendary Talons, the Tribe of the Dragon, the Talis District. But he never imagined, not even in his wildest dreams, he would glimpse, much less have a conversation with one. He believed that they were only myths. But in front of him was living proof that they existed. The man spoke with a commanding tone, "The third one lives in a city. Go to Shodor and you will find her."

Faldor understood what he had to do. Now Hadran could not argue with him taking Ake to Shodor. The Talon jumped up and suddenly wind buffeted them. The wind shut down as abruptly as it had started and they could not see him again.

As they walked back, Garon's dad, who hadn't spoken a word till then, suddenly asked Faldor, "What is a Talon doing in these parts? They don't take part in worldly matters."

"I don't know, my friend. But if a Talon is taking pains in coming so far from his home base, Lasgalan is in serious trouble."

"But what did he mean by 'third one'?"

Faldor did not respond, but looked at back at Ake and Garon, who were ambling behind with the Wolves. He asked

Garon's father, "With your permission, I would like to train Garon along with my nephew."

"All right. Do whatever you feel necessary."

Faldor looked at the four and called out, "Garon, from today, I am going to train you. Bring Edmund along with you." They reached Garon's house, where he and his father went inside to fetch some daggers. Garon returned with his arms filled with daggers. He was wearing a full sleeved shirt, which prevented the daggers from cutting into his skin. He looked at Faldor and said, "Dad insisted." Faldor shrugged and said, "Ake, carry half." They were halfway to the house, when Ake asked Faldor, "How did you find us?"

"Hadver's howl alerted me. As I ran towards where I thought the sound came from, I came across Garon's father and we found you within minutes. He also is a tracker." They came to the house and unloaded the daggers in the garden. Then the two boys and Wolves fooled around till Faldor, Hadran and Hasha came there. Ake wondered why Hasha was also there. He didn't have time to ask her because Faldor and Hadran called them to the centre of the garden. Faldor took two swords and handed one to each of them, saying, "You will be going to Shodor in some time. I have to train both of you with all types of weapons. I will duel Ake, Hadran will duel Garon. Begin."

The two boys circled their opponents, slowly, not moving too fast. Garon suddenly charged at Hadran, keeping his sword pointed back so that Hadran was looking at the hilt. Ake too charged his uncle. He sliced the sword downwards to his uncle's sternum. Faldor saw it coming and thrust his sword towards Ake's undefended stomach, forcing him backwards. His sword's hilt connected with the end of Faldor's blade. Faldor twisted his sword and Ake had no choice but to release the sword. He looked over to Garon, who was also disarmed. He suddenly flicked his wrists outwards and was gripping two daggers, which must have been hidden in his sleeves. He threw one at Hadran's sword, which dropped to the ground. Ake wondered how much force was packed in that one shot. Hadran was now defenceless and Garon still had one dagger in his hand.

Next, Faldor took a piece of cloth and tied it on their eyes. He gave them daggers and asked them to throw them at sandbags ahead of them. Garon went first. He clutched one dagger tightly and threw it at the sandbag. His aim was precise; the dagger went through the bag and out the other end. It was Ake's turn. He threw the dagger. It flew sideways and landed near Hasha's feet. Hadran then spoke, "The sandbag is simple. Now you try the boards." Two boards of dimensions two feet by one foot were placed near the bags. The result was the same as before. Faldor looked at Hadran, pointed to Garon and said, "We found our first Chosen One."

Next, they had to listen to a sound and thrust their sword in that direction. Here also, they were blind-folded. Ake heard the movements and thrust that way. Out of fifty attempts, he got forty-nine correct while Garon got only seven. Hadran smiled sadly and said, "Second Chosen One found."

After lunch, Ake and Garon were resting in the garden, under the apple tree, when they heard the two brothers talking. Some words carried towards them, "…. know what this means. They will restore balance…." Garon turned towards Ake and asked, "Your sister has been watching me for some time now. Any idea why?" Ake shook his head, though he knew the answer. However, when he glanced to his sister's window, she was not there. He wondered how Garon could see that far; Hasha's window was fifty metres away.

A month of training had led to Ake and Garon developing a bond of close friendship. Ake had tried to convince his sister to tell the family about her feelings for Garon, but she wouldn't listen. "At least tell the family. You can tell Garon later."

One day, the boys were woken up well before dawn. Ake rubbed his eyes and looked out the window. They had two hours before the sun rose. In fifteen minutes, they were dressed in warm clothes and in the garden. Nights in Lasgalan were always cool, but just before dawn was the windiest and coldest time. Faldor and Hadran were waiting for them. Faldor smiled at the duo and whistled. Hadver and Edmund came out of the house, the cold weather not bothering them. Faldor then said, "You two have five minutes to hide in the woods. After that, the Wolves will find you. Your task is to stay in the woods without the Wolves getting you. Stay there till dawn and then come back here. We'll be waiting for you. Now go." Ake and Garon ran to the woods and plunged into them. The woods were so dark that Ake would have walked into ten trees had Garon not pulled him out of the way. How he saw them, Ake didn't know. It was as if the woods were one black curtain. They ran a considerable distance inside before Garon suggested that they split up to make it difficult for the Wolves. Just then, Ake heard a faint howl and realised that the Wolves were coming for them. They parted ways and Ake sped onwards. He came to the clearing where they had first encountered the Talon and raced across it. He ran till he felt the ground gradually incline. He kept going up and saw mist forming around it. Nothing unusual, he thought. He came to the top of the incline and saw nothing but mist. He couldn't see more than a few feet ahead. He decided to wait there for some time. Soon, he heard a metallic sound coming in front of him. He stood up and called into the mist, "Is someone there?"

Almost instantly, a robed figure on a Horse charged out of the mist, his hand holding a lance aimed right at Ake's heart.

CHAPTER 7

Ake stood rooted to his spot in fear. He watched the figure get closer. He wanted to run, but his legs would not move. He saw the point of the lance getting closer and closer. He heard a soft growl and could suddenly move. He jumped to his left and saw a red figure jump on the man. The Horse collapsed under the extra weight and the man lost his grip on the lance as Edmund tried to bite the man's neck. But the robe hindered him. The man pushed Edmund away and drew a sword from inside his robes. He pointed it at Edmund, forgetting about Ake, and threw it at the Wolf. Edmund moved to the side and let the sword shoot past him, down the side of what Ake now thought was a hill. Hadver shot out of the mist, jumped on the man, and before anyone could react, put his teeth into the man's neck, killing him and crushing the bones of the neck with an audible crunch. Ake looked at Hadver and was thankful for the Wolves being there to kill the man.

Ake walked to the robed man and immediately smelt smoke, which he saw was coming out of the openings on the robes. He sensed something was wrong and ran down the hill, shouting to the Wolves to do the same. They had barely gone thirty metres when there was a loud explosion behind them and they were propelled another ten metres. Ake felt a heavy weight on his back and collapsed onto the ground. He said, "Whoever it is, get off." He felt the weight reduce and got to his feet. He faced the Wolves and said, "Well, you caught me. Should we go home?" They walked back down and came to the clearing. Garon was entering from the other side. He took one look at the Wolves and ran the way he came. Ake and the Wolves chased him. He had a reasonable head start, but the canines closed the gap fast. Garon took the toughest route, hoping to slow down the trio, but the Wolves were not affected. They caught up with him and Edmund jumped on to him, pinning him down. Fortunately, no harm came to either the boy or the beast. Garon got up and the four of them walked back to the house. On the way, Ake told Garon about what had chanced in the mist. Garon stared at Edmund and asked Ake, "Are you sure it was Edmund who jumped the man? Sometimes, he doesn't even come to greet me when I come back from somewhere."

"Yeah, I am pretty sure it was Edmund." Ake replied. They came out of the woods and walked to the house. By now, the sun had risen. They jumped over the fence and went inside the house. They saw Hadran and Faldor sitting at the table talking to the women.

"They have to go to Shodor. They have no choice, and frankly, neither do we. If we want to save Lasgalan, we need to put our unquestioning faith in them. They are our only hope," Faldor was saying. He turned when he realised that Hasha's eyes had flicked behind him.

"What's going on? Why do you feel Lasgalan needs to be saved?" Garon asked him.

"Second question first. You may not know, but Lasgalan is facing dark days. Someone or something is spreading its dark influence over the land. We need a group of people to fight this influence, before it destroys our way of life. This group are twenty-four teenagers, four from each District, with their own unique abilities, trained by the Talons of the Dragon District."

"Whoa, whoa. Back up, Faldor. How are twenty-four teenagers supposed to fight against an influence? That is like fighting something you can't see."

"Adults think like that. But the reality is that, for a child or teenager, anything is possible. That is why teenagers are needed."

"And what is this "influence" that is darkening Lasgalan?"

"We all know that King Rendaf's father killed Yedgal, the tyrant. I, for one, have reason to believe that he was powerful enough to set up a Tribe, secretly, which would continue his dark ways and slowly return Lasgalan to its former state under him."

Ake and Garon stood mystified and Faldor told them to go to their room. Ake left the door open a crack so that they could hear what was being said, even if it was faint. Ake suddenly thought of something and turned to Garon. "Faldor said three teenagers, right? The Talon told him that the third one would be found in Shodor." He looked at Garon, waiting for him to connect the dots. Garon's eyes widened in realisation. Ake smiled and said, "We are two of the twenty-four of the group." Garon said, "We must have some unique ability. Faldor said so." Ake had already guessed at theirs. "I have super sharp hearing abilities. You can see into the distance and can probably see through objects."

Garon smiled and said, "How do you think I hit my targets blindfolded? Though the blindfold allowed some light through and I was able to see through it easily."

Ake laughed and threw a pillow at him; Garon's staying in his house for a month had led to him and Ake living in the room together. They gave each other space and rough-housed from time to time. They would stare out of the window and try to guess how many stars were in the sky. The Wolves would enter at odd hours, waking them up and falling flat on them in a playful manner, immobilising them. Hasha came in sometimes to talk with them, Edmund jumping on her almost all the time. It took both the boys an effort to lift him off her, Hasha pushing him from under at the same time. He was heavy, but it was more bone than fat under his fur. Faldor came into the room just then and said, "Both of you have a half-hour to eat breakfast and relax. We will be doing some different training today."

Ake did not like the way Faldor's eyes twinkled when he said the word "different". Nevertheless, he and Garon got up and nearly ran down the stairs. They came to the table and looked at their breakfast, not knowing what to start with. There was egg, beef, mutton, duck ham, milk, bread, bananas, oranges and cheese. The boys looked at Faldor, silently asking a question. Faldor said, "Eat up. You will need all your energy for what you will do in this next week or two." He walked out to the garden where Hadran was standing. The boys finished their food and went to the garden.

Faldor was waiting for them. As they walked up to him and Hadran, Ake felt their feet scrape against something in the ground. He heard a soft sound and hit the ground. A branch came out of nowhere and hit Garon in the chest. Ake got up and helped Garon get to his feet. The latter looked at Hadran and asked, "What was that?" Faldor smiled and replied, "This next part of your training is about trusting your instincts. The next two weeks will be all about it. Ake had the right idea to stop and duck. In battle, your instincts will keep you alive." Ake looked at the garden and saw that the two brothers had left it almost bare. He saw a few pieces of wood among the grass. Hadran said, "Walk from here to that end of the garden."

Garon, not suspecting anything, walked towards the other end of the garden. He had hardly taken ten steps when a man popped out of the ground and hit Garon on the head. At least, that's what Ake saw. It was actually a man painted on a piece of wood. Ake understood what they had to do. He walked in the same direction as Garon and stepped on the grass very carefully. He suddenly broke into a run, dodging the "men" as fast as they popped up. He reached the end of the garden and looked back. He had dodged fifteen of those dummies. Garon looked at him, wide-eyed. Ake had no idea how he had managed to do that. Faldor shouted for him to come back. When both the boys came back, he said, "I will give you two sacks. Carry them through the woods for an hour without letting them touch the ground." He gestured to two sacks on the grass near him. They went up to the bags and looked inside. There were only rocks inside. Garon turned to Hadran and asked, "Is this a joke? How can we carry this for an hour?"

"You will be able to. Besides, the Wolves will be going with you. Whenever you try to put the sack down, they will make sure it stays above the ground." Ake looked at Garon and told him, "Do we really have a choice?" They took one sack each and walked towards the woods. Hadver and Edmund followed them and walked ahead of them in a faster pace, forcing the boys to keep up. Within five minutes, the boys were drenched in sweat. Ake looked at Garon, whose broad back reduced the pressure exerted by the sack on it. Ake's back and arm muscles were screaming for mercy as they kept the sack aloft. He leaned against a tree for a few minutes. Garon looked around and said, "We are being watched, Ake. Don't make any sudden moves."

Ake strained his ears and sure enough, heard a faint twig snap and a leaf crackle as someone put his foot on it. Edmund moved protectively towards Garon while Hadver did the same for Ake, both canines growling softly. The two boys stood back-to-back and scanned their surroundings and saw twenty men, all dressed in pink robes, walking towards them. Ake realised that the Wolves would not be able to take down all of them before either Garon or himself were killed. They had two options: stand and fight, with a possibility of death; or they could run and let the robed men give chase. The only problem was that neither of the boys liked to run from a fight. Edmund growled in warning at the men, but they paid no heed to it. In perfect unison, the men drew swords and advanced towards them. With no weapons, the boys were sitting ducks. Ake considered throwing the rocks from the sacks, but they would be too heavy for him to pick up, let alone throw.

But he had forgotten about the Wolves. Hadver and Edmund jumped the men closest to them and brought down eight down before anyone could react. The remaining advanced slowly, wary of the Wolves now. Hadver's tail was still, as it was when he was angry. He bared his teeth at the men and let out a howl so loud that Ake's eardrums were close to breaking. Out of desperation, he picked up a rock from the sack and threw it at one of the robed figures. It was not much of a throw, but the man was caught by surprise and the rock knocked him unconscious. Garon took a step backwards and pulled a rock out of his own sack. He threw it at man in front of Edmund. This one was dodged with ease. Ake realised that there was only one option left, one which he and Garon both hated. He picked up another rock, one significantly larger than the rest, and the men backed away. Ake hoped they didn't know what he knew: he could hold the rock for about a minute. He threw it in front of him, creating an obstacle for the men.

Then he, Garon and the Wolves took off. They heard heavy footsteps of the men running, but didn't dare look behind. The boys' energy was spent in carrying the sacks and could barely put some distance between themselves and the men. Edmund and Hadver seemed to be running in a direction that took them deeper and north into the woods. They saw a tree that looked climbable but it was too short. They kept running and it became darker. They seemed to be running into the older, unexplored part of the woods. They saw trees almost thirty metres tall, the tallest that Ake had seen in his life. They ran past a small stream and jumped across it. Garon risked a glance behind and saw that their pursuers had sheathed their swords and two of them had drawn bows with arrows nocked in them. They were making an arc around the boys and coming up on their sides. The others were still far away, at least fifty metres away and seemed to be slower runners than the archers. Garon suddenly had an idea.

As the archers let go of the strings, he ploughed into Ake, pushing him onto the ground. The arrows whizzed above them, and cut into the archers' necks. Ake and Garon got up and kept running. By now, they were sure that they were lost. But the Wolves seemed to know where they running. Ake heard a faint noise, like running men. He knew that they still had nine men behind them and ran with whatever energy he had left. The noise increased behind them and Ake felt as if they were seconds away from certain death. Sadly, for the men, the Wolves knew exactly where they were running. As the four of them ran into a clearing, they saw Faldor, Hadran and Garon's father facing them, bows drawn and arrows nocked, ready to fire. The boys fell to the ground and all hell was let loose. The nine men were a pincushion for the arrows. They tried to get up and run, but they were losing blood too fast. Faldor put them out of their misery fast with his sword, save one. He pulled the man's hood back to reveal a bald head and a face that betrayed no fear. Faldor looked at him and asked, "Who sent you?"

The man spoke in a raspy voice, "You will lose, Wolf. He will return, and when he does, he will reward us and kill all of you. His wrath is inescapable." So saying, the man raised his head and shouted loudly in a language that Faldor evidently recognised. He ran from the man and so did everyone else. They heard a loud bang behind them and saw that the man and his comrades had been incinerated, a column of fire erupting from within their robes.

CHAPTER 8

Faldor looked at the column of fire erupting from where the man he was interrogating had just been. Ake realised that this group must be the same as the man who tried to kill him in the morning before Edmund and Hadver finished him. So, he saw no harm in telling them what had transpired in the morning. His father looked at him carefully, as if seeing him for the first time. Hadran chose his next words carefully and asked Garon's father, "Can your son come to Shodor next month with us?"

"Yes, he can. I'm coming with you." That question being answered, they walked away from there. Soon, they were back in the sunlit side of the woods. They took an hour or so to reach the house. By then, it was nearly mid-day, the hottest time of the day in Lasgalan. As the seven of them came into the house, Sisha, Fradki, Hasha and a woman who Ake took to be Garon's mother swarmed them to check for injuries that could be infectious. The Wolves went to their favourite spot and sat down on the ground. Hadran and Faldor went to one corner of the room and talked quietly while Garon's father assured his wife that Garon was okay.

Ake suddenly realised something. He walked to Faldor and asked him, "How did you know where to find us?" Faldor smiled at his nephew.

"I had two of the best trackers in Logder with me."

"No, how did you know where exactly we would end up?"

Faldor hated lying, but said, "The howl alerted us and as we came into the woods, Garon's father found us and soon we came to the sacks. There we found the first bodies. The Wolves had obviously made short work of them. Then I remembered that, when threatened, Wolves instinctively go for dark surroundings. So, we ran towards what we thought to be the dark side of the woods. We never realised that they were so expansive."

Ake saw that he was not going to get answers, so he gave up questioning and went to the table and started to eat an apple. Garon's mother looked at him and smiled. Ake smiled back. She asked him, "How long have you known my son?" Surprised, Ake said, "I've known him about seven years, but I have visited your house only once or twice." Glancing towards the brothers, Ake saw that they were having an intense talk in hushed tones. Hadran showed something to Faldor in his hand, the latter looking at it with shock writ all over his face. He glanced at the Wolves and stared hard at them. Without looking at the youths, he said, "We will continue training after lunch. Till then, rest." Both the boys, up for nearly seven hours now, went to the garden and lay down on the ground under the apple tree. They talked about how weird the day had been and wondered what else Faldor had in store for them. They closed their eyes and only opened them when they were called in, the weather being a little hot and windy. They sat down on the ground near the bed and waited for lunch.

They were called down for lunch soon. As they were eating, they saw Faldor sparring outside with Hadran. They finished lunch and went out into the garden. Faldor and Hadran had changed into sleeveless shirts and were looking at the boys expectantly. Without warning, they charged. Ake was taken by surprise and could barely raise a defence before his uncle ploughed into him. Faldor caught him around the waist and, using his momentum, tried to get Ake flat on the ground. However, Ake held his ground and tried to bring his elbow down on Faldor's back. This didn't really affect Faldor, but his grip loosened. Ake managed to wriggle out and, while Faldor was getting up, jumped over him, putting his hands on the latter's back, forcing him down. Faldor hit the ground and Ake jumped on him, hoping Faldor would stay down.

However, the latter swung his arm back hoping to backhand Ake. Ake got off and saw that, with no sleeves, Faldor could swing his arm in a greater arc than himself. He needed to get inside that arc. He thought of the opening move Faldor had used on him and tried that. Faldor caught him by the stomach and picked him up using little effort. Ake felt his stomach do a flip and realised that he was close to losing his lunch. He tried one trick he had seen once in Adnanam. He ran to Faldor and jumped hard. He used the jump to put his legs around Faldor's neck, trying to bring him down. It worked. Faldor fell on the ground and hit Ake's legs, signalling to him to release his hold on his neck.

Ake looked at his father and Garon. Garon was out of his weight division but he was holding on. He didn't try to attack; he kept dodging Hadran, letting the latter stumble past him. He launched himself at Hadran, jumping at the last moment and flipping, so that he kicked Hadran in the chest. The latter hit the ground hard. Once he got up, Faldor, with a smile said, "You have managed to take us out, so now comes the next level." Ake wondered what his uncle was talking about. Faldor went inside and came out with the Wolves. Garon looked at Faldor and asked, "Are you mad? We are out of our weight class here. The Wolves only have to sit on us and that will be the end of the fight."

Faldor smiled and said, "I leave you guys to figure that out." So saying, the two brothers went into the house. The Wolves looked at the boys, and jumped. A month of training had sharpened the boys' reflexes as they crouched and let the canines fly over them. They turned to face them again. Now, the Wolves circled them, slowly waiting to strike. Ake remembered that Hadver was strong enough to bring down a Lion or a Bull. Edmund suddenly charged Garon and jumped on him, flattening the fifteen-year old. Garon struggled to get him off, but the Wolf went limp, leaving the former incapacitated. Hadver ran at Ake at full speed leaving Ake, with his sharp reflexes, on the ground in a second. Faldor came out, clapping, "It seems you were right, Garon; they only had to sit on you."

"Oh, very funny, Faldor," Garon replied. "Now Edmund, get off." The speaker got up and dusted himself while Faldor stretched. Hadran came out and scratched Hadver behind his ears, something he loved. Faldor called the boys and the Wolves to one end of the garden and said, "We will race from here to Garon's house, through the woods. Hadran, please start us off."

Hadran came to the starting point, waited a few seconds before shouting, "Go!" Ake and Garon took off. The Wolves would overtake them in the woods, so they needed to put some distance between them before that. They jumped the fence and opened up. But they forgot about Faldor. He ran past them, the Wolves behind them. They plunged into the woods which hindered Faldor somewhat. Here, the Wolves let loose. They shot past the boys in a blur of dark grey and red so fast Ake and Garon could not even react to them. They closed in on Faldor fast and overtook him. In spite of being last in the race, the teens pushed harder and slowly came up to Faldor who, Ake realised, could only run short bursts at top speed; he had no stamina. As the latter saw the boys overtaking him, he tried in vain to sprint faster. After two minutes of starting, the boys reached the halfway point. The Wolves were barely visible to them now, some sixty metres ahead of them. They had no way of catching up to them; they raced themselves instead. In one minute, they saw the woods coming to an end; they had reached Garon's house. The Wolves exited and the boys and Faldor emerged in another minute.

Garon's father was waiting for them. As the trio emerged, he smiled at them and said, "Took you long enough. The Wolves have already lapped up two litres of water. Fast drinkers, I must say."

Faldor looked at him and said, "We head for the capital in a week. The Games are a month away." Garon asked his father, "Are you also coming?" His father nodded. The five racers slowly walked back.

Chapter 9

Ake got out of the carriage that had transported Garon's family and his own, save Edmund, Fradki and Hadver, to the capital of Logder. Like all other Districts, Logder's capital didn't have a name, and like all cities and towns in Logder, it was fortified. Walls rose to heights of thirty to forty feet, topped with watchtowers from where archers would shoot down any enemy. He saw their District's Lord's palace in the distance on a small hill, on whose highest spire was the banner of the First Wolf, Lord Logdan.

Hadran and Faldor led the way while Garon's father brought up the rear. The only ones missing were Edmund, Fradki and Hadver, who were back in their respective houses. They walked to a building where a line was formed. They stood in line and Faldor explained, "This is where we register you for the Games. After that, we go to Shodor for them." Ake looked around to pass his time; they had about five minutes before they made it to the front of the line. That's when he saw her.

Coming out of a carriage was a girl, not older than himself. She had blonde hair and dark eyes, like Garon and himself. Her hair spilled onto her shoulders, like a curtain. Her face was mask of emotion. She had a wheat-like complexion and long, thin fingers. Ake was brought back to reality by Garon. "Come on, Ake. The line's moving." Taking one last glance at her, the former moved along. When they reached the end of the line, they saw a man writing something in a book. Faldor said, "Ake and Garon. Axe and dagger." The man wrote that in his book, looked up to assess the two boys, and shouted behind him, "One medium and one large. Please go inside."

The group went inside into a room where they saw racks after racks of swords, daggers, axes, knives, clubs, maces, hammers, bows and arrows, spears and javelins, all of different sizes, colours and woods. There were fifteen men stationed around the room. One of them handed the boys two packets saying, "These are your armours. Wear them during the Games and they will keep you alive. Do you need any weapons?" Ake was eyeing a grey bow, but Faldor said, "No, we don't." As they left the room, Ake turned to look for the girl who he saw outside, but heard her voice instead. It was like the sound a bird on the first day of spring. "Do I need a new sword, or will the old one work for now?" He couldn't see her, but hearing her voice was enough. He held his armour up and walked to the carriage, putting it with the other luggage, their weapons and clothes. Faldor said, "It will be short route to the border and then on to Shodor." That being said, they got in the carriage and headed out of the capital.

CHAPTER 10

The carriage reached the border. A man came out of the office and walked around the carriage. He then asked Faldor, "Going for the Games?" Faldor nodded. "I wish you the best. The fighting is becoming more competitive now. The Horses are making a comeback and the Bulls are being coached by their General."

Faldor thanked the man for his advice and the carriage moved on. In a few hours, it became dark and they came to a rest house. The carriage was taken into a room with others. The eight of them went into three rooms, two for the respective families and one for Ake and Garon. The boys sat on the bed and talked in general. Ake asked Garon, "Do you think the Games will be tough?" Garon shrugged. He popped a few grapes in his mouth and said, "No idea. But I hear that they last only until one person is left standing. He or she is declared the best fighter of Lasgalan for that year. My dad said that, last year, the fighting was so fierce that the Games continued for three days. But the Games is the single most watched event in any District in Lasgalan. It is supposed to be only one day of fighting and the rest of the days are competitive fighting. As in, archers face off against each other; javelin and spear wielders see who can throw the farthest, and with how much accuracy.

Things like that." Ake went to the door and locked it. Saying goodnight to Garon, he crawled into his bed and went to sleep.

Next morning, they were up at dawn. Changing their clothes, they went down for breakfast, where the others were waiting for them. Hadran then spoke, "We will leave for Shodor after an hour. Once we reach, the two of you will be on your own." The last statement was directed at Ake and Garon. Soon they were on the road again. There were two types of roads in Lasgalan, cobblestone and metalled roads. The latter were roads that were a little more protected than the former; otherwise, they were the same.

They reached Shodor in the evening. As they got down from the carriage, Garon noticed the difference between the cities of Logder and Tauris. Logder's cities had watchtowers where archers could shoot from whereas Shodor, a Taurian city, had holes in the walls from where hot oil could be dropped to burn the enemy trying to scale the wall. Meanwhile, a heavy-set man came up to them and exchanged a few words with Faldor. He then turned to the boys and said, "I will escort you to your room. Please get all your belongings and follow me." He led them into a small building which had a Wolf statue on top of its door. Ake looked back to see the other carriages bringing the other contestants from the three other Districts; Talis never took part in the Games. The man guided them through a corridor to a room. He turned and said, "This is a room only for blade wielders; I understand that you prefer blades for weapons. There are three other rooms for Wolves, each for different weapons." Ake and Garon went inside the room and saw five sets of bunk beds, four of which were occupied by two boys and six girls. Garon went to the last set and jumped onto the top one. Ake put his belongings under his bed. Garon took his armour out of his bag opened it and examined it carefully.

The armour itself was blue and grey, the colours of Logder. Underneath it was a chainmail which would act as a last defence against any attack, if the armour broke. The helmet had a blue plume, probably to distinguish the District in combat. A face of a Wolf was embossed in the centre of the chest. The arm and leg guards were black. Putting it aside, Garon told Ake, "Tomorrow we have to do some training by ourselves since Faldor won't be there." But Ake was not listening to him. He was trying to pinpoint the location of the girl from the capital as he could hear her voice though it was faint even for him. Because of this power and what he was currently using it for, Ake felt a bit like a stalker. He turned to Garon and said, "Tomorrow we will get up at dawn and go for a run. Then we do some training." Garon nodded and shifted his pillow to the other side of the bed so that, at dawn, the sun's rays fell on his face through the window. He closed his eyes and was snoring softly in a minute. Ake strained his ears to get the position of the girl as he could still hear her voice.

Finally, he couldn't stand it. He got up and went into the corridor, where he could hear her a bit more clearly. He looked for a room for blades, since he remembered her talking about a sword. He casually walked around and came to a room on top of whose door was inscribed, "BLADES". He cast a casual glance and saw that this room also had five pairs of bunk-beds, all of which had bags on them, but only nine had people either sleeping or talking on them. He was about to move on when he heard her voice.

"Looking for someone?"

Ake spun round and saw her, not more than two feet from him. She was about his height and smelled of mountain pine. Ake had been to almost all the cities of Logder, but no one had captured his heart like she had. He forgot how to speak a complete sentence, but managed to say, "No." She then looked at him for a few awkward seconds before saying, "My name's Elesa."

"Ake."

She was about to say something when her eyes flicked behind Ake and said, "I think your brother is looking for you." She went inside as Ake turned and saw Garon standing at the entrance of their room. Ake walked up to him. Garon raised an eyebrow and said, "You, my friend, have no idea how to talk to a girl."

"Shut up, Garon." Garon laughed and patted him on the back. Steering the latter into the room, he jumped on the bed and said, "You will know what to say when the time comes." Ake sat down and stared out another window, looking at the sun setting behind the trees, casting an orange glow on them. He didn't realise how tired he was until he lay down on his bed and was immediately engulfed by sleep.

CHAPTER 11

Garon woke up in a cold sweat suddenly in the night. He looked around the room to see if he had woken up anyone. He steadied his breathing and thought about his dream. It was a bit scary, and Garon wasn't scared easily. He looked out of the window where the full moon shone like a spot of light in the darkness of the sky. Looking back into the room, he tried to see who was in the bed opposite him. He strained his eyes to see in the almost full darkness of the room. Suddenly, something strange happened.

Everything changed colour. Instead of seeing black, he saw everything in red, yellow, green and blue. The red and yellow outlined the person opposite him. Garon looked around the room and saw everything in the same way. He realised that he was seeing everything from the heat generated by the objects. Remembering reading about snakes once and their ability to see in darkness, Garon realised he was seeing things like a snake probably would. He closed his eyes hard, and when he opened them again, it was normal. Weird, he thought as he shifted his gaze to his feet. Here, however, nothing happened. He breathed a silent sigh of relief and went back to sleep.

Next morning, Garon woke up as the sun shone onto his face. Getting up, he saw that he was the first of the ten in the room to wake up. He slowly got down to the ground and slowly shook Ake awake. Once the latter was up, they quietly opened the door and walked out. The man who had guided them to the room was standing at a door leading to a large field, where the contestants for the Games would be practising. He looked at their approach and said, "There's a bit of fog outside; are you sure you want to practise now?" Garon nodded and the man stepped aside and let them pass. Stepping outside, they saw a thin layer of fog evaporating in the sun. They could see the tracks for jogging and set out on them for some time. Garon wondered if he should tell Ake about the previous night, but decided against it. He suddenly saw through the fog; it was as if the fog became transparent before him. There was a large oak tree with a canopy of considerable size ahead of them, with some acorns hanging from its branches. They kept on jogging to that spot, where Ake said, "That's an impressive tree. I wonder how old it is."

That sentence assured Garon that he had not visualised the tree before. His father always said that Garon had sharp eyes, but this was taking it a bit too far. As they went around the field, Garon saw that there were four other buildings around it. They would be for the other four Districts. From the outside, all five buildings looked the same and housed forty contestants at a time, though that was rare. Slowly, other contestants started to come into the field and do some exercise, whether it was sparring or running or simply stretching. They had been jogging and talking for about two hours, when Ake stopped dead in his tracks. Garon too stopped and followed his gaze. He softly chuckled, "Relax, Ake. If she wants, she will come to you," for Ake was looking straight at Elesa, from across the field. Garon could understand why Ake had fallen for her. She exuded a quiet confidence and did not look as if she was self-conscious, even though she was surrounded by boys in the field.

Garon realised that Ake was probably in love with the girl and asked the former, "What's her name?"

Without hesitation, Ake let the ethereal name roll over his tongue, "Elesa." Unknown to the former, the latter had come out to look for him. When they saw each other, Garon started to say, "You know, I'll just……," when Ake stopped him and said, "Let's go back inside. I am feeling a bit tired." He knew that they would have to cross her to go inside. Garon said, "No, you are staying here. I will get our weapons." So saying, he walked to the door, where Elesa was standing with her friends and wishing them good morning, went inside the Wolves' building. As he went into their room, he heard a soft step. He didn't have to be an expert to know that whoever made soft steps was most likely not a good person. He grabbed a dagger from his bag and peeked into the corridor, where he saw at least five pink-robed figures coming out of the first room at the other end of the corridor. He stood in plain view and shouted, "Hey!" The men turned to face him and pointed their swords at him. One said, "Surrender to us, youngling, and we will give you a quick death." Garon knew he could not take them all on himself, so he said, "Well, I have no fancy in dying today so why don't you go back to where you came from?" The men snarled at him and charged.

Throwing his dagger at one of them, he ran. A painful shout told him that he hit his target and he ran up some stairs. He didn't know where he would end up, but knew he had to keep them away from the contestants. He ended up in a room full of bags of grain and stood his ground. In a moment, the four men were facing him. He crouched, ready to take them on with his bare hands if it came to that. He saw movement behind them and suddenly a sword sliced into the one at the back. Distracted by the new entity, the other three men turned away from

Garon. This was all he needed. He ran to the one closest to him and pushed him down, hard. The man died instantly. The others were cut down by the sword wielder. Facing the person, Garon saw that it was none other than Elesa. He said, "Thanks Elesa."

"No problem, my friend. Although you could tell me who you are."

"My name's Garon. How did you find me?"

"I was going to my room when I heard someone running. So I followed the sound and came up the stairs and ran into those guys. Who are they, do you know?"

Garon thought carefully and said, "I've had a couple of run-ins before with them, but I have no idea who they are." They started walking down the stairs and reached Garon's room, where he grabbed two daggers and Ake's axe. Elesa looked at the axe and said, "Do you like an axe or daggers?"

"Oh, daggers. The axe is my friend's."

"Is his name Ake?"

"Yes."

Elesa looked at him as they came out of the building and said, "I thought he was your brother."

Garon laughed and said, "Yes, I suppose most people think that." He saw Ake sitting under tree watching them approach. He turned to Elesa and asked her, "You want to spar with us?" Elesa said, "No thanks. I have my group to practise with." So saying, she walked to her friends while Garon went to Ake and tossed him the axe. Ake asked him, "What took you so long? And why was Elesa with you?"

"Long story my friend. But it involved five of those bald guys who are probably the last king's men." Ake stared at him with wide eyes and said, "If they can slip into Shodor like that without being spotted, we will have to be careful. We still need to find the third one. We only know it's a she."

"I think it is Elesa. It has to be, Ake. No other Wolf has blonde hair and dark eyes together, here. It's either one or the other, and she is the only one with both."

"Maybe. But how do we know that she knows about the Legend? We don't and that's the problem." Just then, a few men came into the field and announced that breakfast was ready. Everyone went into their own buildings and were guided to the first floor. The eating room was large enough for hundred people, not merely just thirty of them (Garon had counted them). As they sat down, a man came up and spoke to the group, "Your breakfast lasts for an hour, so don't eat in a hurry. The field is closed from sunset, so don't try to hide so you can train after that; we will find you. The Games begin tomorrow, so I wish you all the best." With that said, he left the room and ten others started to go around and serve the food to the hungry youths. Throughout the meal, Garon saw that, when Ake was not looking, Elesa was staring at either Ake or himself. He silently laughed at the fact that Ake might be in love with Elesa, but what he didn't know was that the converse was also true. Ake and Garon finished their breakfast in half an hour and went down to the room to relax before the mid-morning training session. They crashed on their beds and Ake asked Garon, "What exactly happened with, you know, his men?" Garon related the incident and after that, Ake smiled and said, "Guess it is good to have a sword-wielding Wolf other than Faldor around when you're being hunted." Garon laughed and said, "Yes, I suppose it is."

Then it happened again. The world shifted in Garon's eyes. But this time, it was not any change in colour, it was as though he was looking at the oak tree; he could see right through the room wall into the corridor. And who should be standing outside the door, listening to their conversation, but Elesa herself. He saw her trying to listen through the wall but sadly, she didn't possess Ake's abilities and had to stand close to the door to listen. Garon rummaged through his bag and pulled out a dagger. All his daggers were sheathed and he had about a hundred of them in his bag. He had two bags, one for clothes and one for weapons and his armour, which he had kept near the wall openly.

He smiled and said, "We will go for training in an hour and a half. Till then you want to play some games?" Ake replied, "Sure, what do you have?" So, for the greater part of their break, they were playing cards. Their parents had told them that they could play cards, but never to play with wagers and money; that was regarded as gambling and families had been ruined by it. Out of the ten games they played, Garon won seven and Ake had won only three. While they were playing the final game, Ake tensed. Garon saw this and instinctively went for his dagger. Ake set down his deck down slowly and signalled to Garon to pass the axe. While doing this, Garon unsheathed his dagger and looked at Ake, asking him a silent question as to where the sound came from. Ake pointed to the door and Garon tried to see who was there and saw a hulk of a man walking past the door towards the field. On his back was a shirt with the face of a Bull on it. Realising it was a helper for the Games, Garon put his dagger down and signalled for Ake to do the same.

Realising his mistake, Ake put his axe down and they continued the game, Ake winning this one. They got ready for the next session of training and walked out. Since their roommates had not come in since breakfast, they closed the door and went to the field. Garon saw that probably all the contestants had come out to train and that it was going to be tough trying to train. Nevertheless, they went to the less crowded part of the field and stretched a bit. They readied their weapons and fought. They were not the only ones doing so; there were at least twenty other groups doing the same. Ake used his axe as a defence against the small daggers, but every now and then, Garon penetrated his defence and managed to hit him with the blade.

Next, they decided to wrestle. Keeping their weapons close, they gripped each other's shoulders and wrestled. Garon had the advantage as he was taller. But Ake was smaller and more agile. Out of every five times Garon tried to grab him, Ake escaped at least twice. Ake then suggested they put their weapons back and race. Doing that, they decided to race two laps of the field. They started running at top speed and overtook some other runners. By the time one lap was over, Garon was a metre ahead of Ake and both were sprinting as hard as they could. As the finish was coming near, they were neck and neck. They crossed the line together while, unknown to them, Elesa was watching them. As they caught their breath, two boys from Covis, the Raven District, came up to them and one of them said, "We are the fastest runners under twenty-one in our District. Will you race us?"

Garon looked at their arms, which had tattoos of Ravens on them and said, "Fine. But can we know your names? I am Garon and this is Ake."

The boy who had spoken said, "I'm James and this is Chris."

"Fine, lets race. One lap of the field per person." Ake started with James and Garon shouted, "Go." The two boys shot down the track at breakneck speed, Ake in the lead, in spite of having raced with Garon a few minutes before. As they came to the halfway point, James pulled ahead, ever so slightly. They were like this till they finished their lap. Their counterparts waited for them to come and sprinted away. Despite having an advantage, Chris was getting caught by Garon, and fast. Garon charged ahead, but Chris was up to the challenge. At the halfway mark, Garon was ahead by ten metres and Ake told James, "Your friend is going to need a miracle to win this race. Garon is way too fast for him."

James smiled at Ake and said, "He doesn't need one, Ake; he is one." Wondering what he meant, Ake turned back to the race where Garon was still leading. That's when Chris burst. He accelerated so fast, Ake thought he was possessed. By the time they had a quarter lap left, he had overtaken Garon and probably raised the temperature of the grass he was running on by a degree or so. He finished the race five metres ahead of Garon and smiled at Ake and said, "Fastest runner in Covis, under twenty-one." Ake looked at Garon and asked, "What in the name of Lord Logdan was that?" Garon said, winded, "It's not as easy as it looks. His last burst caught me by surprise. Once I realised what was happening, it was too late."

"Still, it was a good run," Chris' voice said. "I haven't had competition like that in two years." They faced the runners, who were smiling at them in a way that made them feel as if they were praiseworthy. "How old are you guys, anyway?" Garon asked them.

"Oh, I am sixteen and James here is fourteen. You?"

"Ake is fourteen and I am fifteen."

Ake looked at James' hands which were crossed over his chest. He had a knife in his belt and his hand was just inches away from it, as if he expected an attack any moment. Ake asked Chris, "What weapon do you prefer?" Without hesitation, the former answered, "A mace. I've always liked big, heavy things to hit with, so I chose a mace. I saw you guys practising with an axe and dagger. Lovely choice of weapons." He wasn't even sounding sarcastic. They sat on the ground, talking about their lives in their respective Districts when Ake saw Elesa looking at them. She was staring right at him, and Ake felt as if he was Hasha and Elesa was Garon, including the fact that Garon didn't know about Hasha's crush on him.

Suddenly, James asked them, "Can you guys climb that tree?" He pointed to the oak tree which was not very far away. Garon laughed and said, "Whoever can climb it would be a daredevil. It's near impossible." The tree itself was about sixty feet of twisted trunks and branches. One round of the base was about a hundred feet, the lowest branch being a little more than eight feet high. One wrong step could lead to someone falling to his or her death. Laughing, Chris said, "This time tomorrow, we will be on opposing sides. The last one standing will have a choice of a challenge." Seeing the Wolves' confused faces, he explained, "The last one standing has a choice of who he wants to challenge; the challenged person will be a person who has won the Games before. This year is the first year they are doing it. They are bringing the last thirty years' winners."

Ake and Garon looked at Chris in silence. To be the last one standing would be a dream come true, but to fight someone who had won the Games before was something else altogether. They spent the rest of the morning talking to each other about different weapons and who might win the Games by looking at different contestants. When it got too hot, they went into their respective buildings and it gave them time to cool down before lunch. Garon wondered if fighting Chris would be a good idea considering he wielded a mace. Also, his speed would come into play tomorrow and help him dodge all his attackers as well as him being the attacker. Thinking about this, he lay down on his bed and closed his eyes till they were called for lunch.

CHAPTER 12

James always had a way of making friends by finding some common ground between himself and the person concerned. As he walked back to the room that Chris and himself shared with eight others, he thought about the new friends he had made just a few hours ago. They showed a relaxed attitude as if they had all the time in the world. But he needed to know what they would do if a crisis arose and they had to deal with it. He came into the room, went to his bed and awaited lunch. Soon, they were called and everyone in the building went to the next floor where the dining room was. Though the Ravens were thirty-five strong, they still fitted in the room with space to spare. During lunch, he kept to himself and ate half a leg of lamb, something he only did if he was really hungry.

He finished his lunch and hurried back to his room to open his armour and let it air out. It was a bit large for him but otherwise it was okay. It was in red and black, Covis' sacred colours. It also had the open beak of a Raven on it. He sat on his bed and looked out of the window to the mid-day sunlit field where he had met his new friends and said to himself, "At least those guys didn't have a Talon writing their destiny." He did not know how wrong he was, for he didn't know that the people concerned were also thinking the same about him and Chris.

The latter came into the room smiling and looked at the melancholy James before saying, "What's wrong, brother?" Though James and he were not blood related, they had a bond that people said, "Was a brotherly bond".

Looking at the smiling Chris, James said, "Ake and Garon are lucky. They don't have all this "accepting your destiny" nonsense to deal with. They're more carefree and laidback, without a fear in the world."

"That they maybe James, but don't forget what that Talon said. Twenty-four of us are required. They could be two of the twenty-four." Chris realised what was troubling James. He sat on his bed and lifted the covers, revealing a polished mace. Unlike Hadran's mace, which was a rod, chain and spiked ball, Chris' was a single piece of metal. It was blood-red in colour and weighed about ten pounds. Most rational people would think twice before taking on a mace-wielding behemoth, but some people wouldn't care. They'd charge Chris, with a chance of getting only a few broken bones. The latter didn't play around with attackers; he swung his mace with deadly effect, taking people out in one or two swings of the mace. He liked to finish his battles as fast as possible. Unlike James, Chris took the Talon's words in stride, without worrying about anything. That was one thing about Chris; he never cracked under pressure, no matter how bad the situation was.

Lying down on his bed, Chris said, "Don't worry about it, James. For all we know, the Talon probably isn't even of this era. He may have mistaken us for some future generation. We might just lead normal lives."

"Then how do you explain the five attacks on us?" There had been five attempts on the duo's lives, all of which they had thwarted. The assassins were always dressed in pink robes and, from one attack, they knew that the assassins were bald.

"Fair point." Chris looked out of the window and sighed. "Well, we're here now. Might as well forget about it, James. We got a lot of people to get out of our way to win the Games. We'll worry about our destiny later." So saying, he went to sleep. James looked at his back and decided to go back to the field so that he could be alone for some time. He walked out of the room as his other roommates came inside. He went into the field and walked to the oak tree where he would get some shade from the sun. Sitting there, he looked towards the tree and a wild idea came to his head, one that he had asked Ake and Garon before. Before he could become rational again, he jumped towards the lowest branch, grabbing it and, swinging himself to another, he stood up on it. Cautiously putting one foot in front of the other, he reached the trunk and holding on for dear life, started to scale it. He reached a height of about twenty feet when he smelt smoke. He looked at the ground but nothing was there. He looked up and his blood froze.

CHAPTER 13

Ake walked into the field to practise his axe wielding on the oak tree, as he knew from old experience that it would take him fifty tries to even make a visible mark on its trunk. He had barely taken five steps when he saw James holding on to the trunk of tree and ten pink-robed men on a branch above him, one of whom was holding a small vial with green liquid in it and was ready to drop it on James. It was also giving off green smoke, which Ake thought was not a good sign.

He sprinted to the tree as two men noticed him and shot arrows at him. Cutting them in half, Ake threw his axe at them, which made the man with the vial pull his hand back for safety. The two closest to him lost their arms and fell to the ground. The others jumped to the ground and surrounded him. Grabbing Ake's axe, which had embedded itself in a branch, James jumped down on the ground and threw it to him. They were outnumbered one to four, and Ake wasn't liking his chances against them. They couldn't call for help as they would be shot down before they could make it to their respective buildings. The man with the vial in his hand was clearly the leader because everyone was looking at him as if waiting for instructions. He looked at James and said, "Kill the Raven. He could have been of use to us, but I need only the Wolf." Ake brandished his axe and said, "Nothing doing. You will die before you lay a finger on James." The man laughed. "Do you know who you are messing with, youngling? It would be better if you just surrender yourself to us along with your other two Wolf friends."

Thanks a lot, you idiot, Ake thought as the man's words confirmed who the third Chosen One from Logder was. James took his knife out of his belt and pointed it at the vial.

"Do I need to guess what will happen if I break that vial or will you tell me?"

"You will never know, youngling, because you will be dead before that. But suffice has it to say that you will cease to exist because your bones will never be recovered."

By now, Ake had enough. He charged the leader and brought his axe down with full force into his chest. The man's grip on the vial loosened as he fell, the vial getting thrown upwards. Ake snatched it out of the air and faced the remaining seven men, whose hoods fell back as they eyed the vial and made no sudden moves. Ake noticed that, these men were not bald like the ones who had chased Garon and himself into the dark parts of the woods near his house. It seemed like it happened just yesterday. They made a wide arc around the two boys, the closest one being ten feet away. James looked at his knife and Ake knew that he could take out only one man before the rest got the opening to kill them. Ake realised that, since he had the vial in hand, they would not risk killing him for fear of the vial hitting the ground and exploding.

Taking a risk, James threw his knife at the man closest to him, who didn't think that the former would actually do something as stupid as that. The others unsheathed their swords and ran to intercept the defenceless James. Ake threw the vial right at them, where it exploded on impact with one of them. A green flash and the two boys were looking at a ground which held no evidence that there were any men present there. The grass was not even charred. Ake looked at James, who had his knife in hand.

"Are you ok, James?"

"I am fine. Just about managed to grab my knife out of the man before you threw the vial. Any idea what was in it?"

Ake shook his head and said, "I know who these men are. Garon and I have nearly been killed by them back in Logder. They used some incantation to burst into flames so that we would be left in the dark as to who they were." He saw that James was looking at him with a very queer expression on his face. "What's wrong, James?"

"I know this is a weird question, Ake, but was there someone before them, called a Talon?"

"Yes, there was. Why?"

"A man claiming to be one came to Chris' house when I was also there. Chris' dad, he and I chased him until we were a considerable distance from the house. He then said that the two of us had some destiny to accept before it was too late and that we would find a third Raven in Shodor."

Ake noticed the similarity in the way the Ravens were drawn out as was himself and Garon. He replied, "The Talon who drew Garon and myself out said the same thing. He said that the third one was a girl."

"Oh, for us it is a boy."

"What is your skill-set," Ake asked without thinking.

"My weapon is a knife and I am quite elusive. Back in Covis, we used to play war games and I was the only spy never to be caught. I did that for three years. So my skill-set is using a knife and being elusive. I know Chris wields a mace, but I don't know if he has a particular power. In the war games, enemies would walk right past me as if I didn't exist. I could have been right in front of them and they'd never notice me. What's yours?"

"I use an axe and my hearing abilities are much sharper than a normal person's. In fact, what I can tell you right now, is what is going on behind the back door of the Wolf's building."

"What is happening?"

"Absolutely nothing, if you exclude the fact that someone is coming out of the Bull's building."

"And Garon's," James asked.

"He uses daggers. His eyesight is good, but I wouldn't call it a power. You better go inside. You will be a bit more protected than if you stayed out here." As Ake said that, a boy walked out of the Bull's building, just as Ake had predicted. He looked as if he had a major growth spurt that not only affected his height, but his arms as well, which looked a bit like Faldor's. He looked about fifteen years old and held a long sword in his hand. He went to the side of the trunk opposite to the boys and swung his sword with such speed that Ake needed a second to adjust his eyes to see the swing. The boy's right forearm had an amulet that covered the entire forearm and had a figure of a Bull embossed on it.

The fourteen-year-olds started walking to their building and Ake asked James, "What are the chances of you taking that guy in a fight?" he pointed back at the sword-slinger.

"Less than zero," came the blunt reply. Laughing, they parted ways and walked back to their buildings and waited for dinner and sleep.

CHAPTER 14

The day dawned. The contestants were woken up and taken to the breakfast table, where scrumptious meals were served to them. They were then instructed to go to their rooms, wear their armour and wait for further instructions. The fifteen-year-old Garon had slept well in the night and was ready for any kind of attack during the Games, after hearing of the ambush on James, and himself escaping from the band of assassins. Still, the chances of an attack happening were not high, as there would be people watching and the security would be tight around the field of play.

He and Ake strapped on their armour, with the help of a manual provided by one of the helpers. Slinging his axe onto his back, Ake sat down on his bed and studied the helmet. Garon pointed his dagger at a tree outside and mimed a throw at it. Turning round, he told Ake, "When we go out there, we have just one aim; get the opposition out of the way and have fun taking each other out. But don't forget, we are just the two of us in a group. Others have groups which are bigger. We will have to be careful."

"Right you are, Garon. Let's see what the layout of the fighting arena is. Then, we will discuss tactics." Garon nodded. Just then, one of their room-mates said, "The two of you will be easy targets. Remain in the thick of the battle and you will be finished. Stay on the outside and go for the kill whenever you get the opportunity. I did that last year and was the fourth last one to be knocked out."

"Thanks man. May we know your name?"

"Jax. I am a good tracker and," leaning in closer said, "I know about the prophecy that concerns you two."

"I'm sorry, I don't know what you are talking about, Jax."

"Hm. Don't act daft, Garon. I know what the Talon told you guys. Yes, I know there's a Talon involved. After all, it was he who placed me here to watch you. And between the three of us, there are others in the other buildings as well. Remember my advice."

Ake looked around their room and saw that the other seven room-mates were not in earshot. A huge Taurian came and announced that the youths could come out. Doing so, they came into the corridor, where the other rooms' contestants were also waiting. Ake spotted Elesa almost instantly, which should have been an indicator as to how strong his crush on her was. There were two other Taurians in the corridor. Since it was about ten feet wide, the corridor did not make anyone squash up against each other.

The contestants were guided through a door they had not seen and walked down a passage that was dark except for torches placed at regular intervals on the wall. They walked for about fifteen minutes before they saw light at the end of the tunnel. They stopped walking as they came to a gate and heard the roar of a crowd. One of their guides said, "This is where we leave you. The gate will open in a few minutes and then you will have to go out. Once outside, wait until you hear a horn blow three times. Only then will you attack. Do not decapitate anyone or cut off any body part."

"I thought the whole purpose if the Games was to get people out of the way and be the last one standing," a voice came from the back of the group.

"Yes, that is correct. However, you do not have to kill them to win. You just have to force them into submission. Or get them on the ground and make sure that they don't get up in a fighting spirit. No matter how badly you injure your opponents, our doctors can heal them back to normal. But do not kill. Is that understood?" The last statement was directed to the whole group, which nodded. "Good. We now leave you. Good luck and may the best fighter win."

The three Taurians left as the Wolves waited for the gate to open. Ake and Garon did a last-minute check on their armours and weapons. Ake asked Garon, "How many daggers do you have?"

"Four. Two are in my hand and two are fastened to the inside of my arm-guards. They are my backup in case anything happens to the main ones." Garon replied, showing Ake two sheathed daggers which were fastened between the inside of his forearms and the straps of his arm-guards.

The gate opened, almost noiselessly. The contestants put on their helmets and walked out into the field. The roar of the crowd seemed to increase tenfold as they came out into the sunlight. Ake looked around and saw that the arena was huge and that the gate which they had just come through was in the shape of the open mouth of a Wolf, just like the one on their armour. The other Districts' contestants were coming through gates shaped in the form of their respective animals. They positioned themselves in front of their gates and waited for the horn to be blown three times. Ake scanned their surroundings to see what could be of advantage to him. There were trees here and there; big rocks had been planted, some of them having a height of fifteen feet. He saw, from the corner of his eye, Garon unsheathe his daggers and throw the sheaths to the ground.

Ake looked around at the taller rocks, judging their defensive advantage. Just then, at a portico above the Horses' entrance, two men emerged. One of them raised his hand and the crowd fell silent. He then said, in a booming voice, "Let the Games begin."

CHAPTER 15

The horns blasted loudly and the crowd roared, drowning out the sound and the five groups charged each other. Ake saw some archers from their group run to the trees closest and climb up, arrows nocked. He saw James and Chris running at full speed at the Lions, knife and mace in hand. Jax led him and Garon behind a tree and said, "What will be of advantage to the both of you are the rocks. Garon, you can stay at the base of the rocks and fling your knives at opponents. Ake, you can run up the rocks, jump down and use your axe to good measure. Don't worry about killing them; all our armours are made to withstand an impact equal to that of a one-ton rock hitting the earth at the speed of one league a minute. The armour will crack after repeated hits of considerable force, but it will not break. Now, I leave you to fight, I too need to survive." So saying, he left, leaving the duo to fend for themselves.

Garon looked around for potential threats. He pointed to a Taurian who was fighting five Equine, "Horse" warriors simultaneously and was, impressively, holding his own, knocking them aside. Ake realised, with icy certainty, that this was the same boy from the previous day, who was slicing away at the oak tree.

Garon asked Ake, "Want to try out what Jax suggested?"

"Might as well."

They ran to the tall rock near the boy and took their positions, just as the last Equine warrior was swatted away. As the Taurian turned, Garon flung his dagger at the boy's shin, hoping to at least distract him while Ake got him from the back.

First problem, the dagger ricocheted off the greave, landing further away from Garon than the latter would have liked. Second problem, as Ake jumped from the top of the rock, aiming to get the Taurian in the back, what he did not see before jumping, was the huge shield on the former's back. It was circular in shape and covered most of his back. The axe glanced off the shield without as much as a scratch on the latter. The boy turned to face Ake. This was all Garon needed. He sprinted for his dagger and left Ake to deal with the sword-wielder. Not fancying his chances, Ake swung his axe at the boy's chest. Not a scratch. Ake was no match for this warrior. He saw someone behind the rock he had just jumped from and saw a mace in the wielder's hand. Seeing a familiar figure jump off the rock, the same rock, he looked at the boy's face and said, "Bye." Chris charged the boy from behind while Ake turned to look for Garon.

He saw the former dive for his own weapon as an arrow passed under his stomach, narrowly missing him. He grabbed the hilt of the dagger and did a full flip, landing on his one knee on the ground in a kneeling position. But Ake could see what Garon couldn't: a girl from Covis was running to Garon's back, her sword poised to cut his shoulder which was slightly exposed beneath his armour. Ake barely had time to shout a warning to Garon, when the latter did the impossible.

His hand flicked back and the dagger shot towards the girl, who couldn't even raise a defence. The distance between the two was about ten feet, but the dagger covered the same in a second or two. As the dagger hit the armour, the latter shattered and the impact propelled the girl backwards into a tree, knocking her unconscious in her chainmail.

Retrieving his dagger, Garon told Ake, "Your uncle is a very efficient teacher; remind me to thank him for showing me that move, once all this is over." Ake nodded and turned, just in time to assess a new threat: another axe-wielding boy from Leonis, the Lion District. He was maybe fourteen years old and five inches shorter than Ake, but his axe looked too heavy for him to carry, let alone swing and hit a target. His first swing nearly decapitated Ake, leaving the latter to reassess the attacker. The boy swung his axe again at Ake's face, forcing him to duck. The blade sliced the plume clean off Ake's helmet. Ake got a lesson that moment; never underestimate your opponent, no matter how big or small they are. As they circled each other, Ake did not realise that he was a target for someone else as well. He suddenly heard Garon scream behind him, in a voice so loud that Ake felt that his friend was dead. Knocking the boy and Garon's attacker out of commission in less than ten seconds, he dragged Garon behind a rock that shielded them from most of the battle.

Garon's triceps were cut badly, and he was losing blood at a slow yet alarming rate. One small door opened behind them and two doctors came to attend to Garon. They removed Garon's helmet and threw water on his face to keep him awake. As they applied pressure on the wound to slow the blood-flow, the incapacitated fifteen-year old grabbed Ake's arm and said, "Sorry I had to leave you like this, but," he coughed up some blood before saying, "you will have to fight on you own now."

Ake realised that, in order to keep Garon in a fighting spirit, he would need to give him some incentive; it was common human nature to work when given incentive. But what incentive could he give Garon? What did Garon not have? That's when Ake made a solemn promise never to lie to his sister again and hoped she would forgive him for what he was about to do. He grabbed Garon's face and turned it so that they were staring into each other's eyes.

"Listen, pal. My sister has a crush on you, so you better get up and fight so that you don't look weak in her eyes."

That was enough. Garon waved away the doctors and got up, bracing himself on his daggers. He took the support of the rock for a few seconds before standing up straight. He looked at Ake and said, "Well, let's fight."

"Spoken like a true Wolf." Ake and Garon jumped back into the battle and for the next half-hour, they knocked people out of the way at a considerable rate. Soon, there were about forty contestants left. Through all the mayhem, the archers had managed to get some targets, but were now sitting ducks as their quivers were either empty or almost there. One of them jumped down from her tree and drew a hunting knife. It looked like it was custom-made, as it had two blades. One was the regular blade, the other was folded into the hilt, where it could be released by some spring mechanism.

By now, the crowd's roar was loud enough to disorient Ake a bit. He looked around to see who was left from Logder, the number being ten. He noticed that the boy who James and Chris had fought after him was still standing. That's when all hell was let loose.

A Taurian who was wielding a club went berserk and launched himself at the Horses, taking out three of them before one of them took him out by a simple fist in the chest, making him fly to a door twenty feet away, where he was carried out by three doctors. Ake looked at Garon and asked, "What was that all about?"

Garon looked at Ake before replying, "The Taurian was a berserker. They can withstand a lot of pain and can go on fighting even if they have a sword in their heart. At least, that's what the Legends say about them. Only a berserker can inflict damage on another. So, that Equine is also a berserker."

The five Districts' warriors were now facing each other in small groups. Ake wondered what the outcome was going to be like and remembered what Garon had said about the Games going on for three days. As he wondered about his next move, he heard the crowd start shouting. He happened to glance up a rock and what he saw nearly stopped his heart.

CHAPTER 16

Garon followed Ake's shocked gaze to the rock, where he saw fifty men, all pink-robed, with different kinds of weapons drawn, ready to slice up the contestants. He called out to Ake, "Hey Ake."

Ake turned to see Garon give him a bored smile. "Never a dull day, is there?"

"Very true."

And with that being said, Ake and Garon did something that was absolutely foolhardy. They charged up the rock. At the same time, unknown to them, their friends from Covis had also decided to storm the rock.

The men didn't react for a few crucial seconds, and that cost them dearly. Five men went down, courtesy of two swings of a heavy mace. No one would have ever tried to attack them, especially when they were outnumbered and had comparatively no experience in fighting. What they did not know was that the four boys who were facing them had been coached by three winners of the Games themselves. The boys were outnumbered about eleven to one, which was dangerous given that the men had more variety of weapons.

The boys formed a wide arc around the men, cutting off their escape and leaving them with one option: stand and fight.

The boy with sharp hearing abilities could hear people running through the tunnels. So, reinforcements were on the way. The men could jump down and knock everyone else out, but trained warriors were probably more than a match for them. And Ake was sure that almost everyone in the stadium was handy with their own weapon. Before they could make a move, one of the archers lifted his bow and pointed it skywards, the nocked arrow having an orange flame. As he released it, there was a screeching sound and then a loud bang. Ake covered his ears as the noise was too much for his enhanced hearing; the sound was magnified by his "sensitive ears", as Garon had once called them.

"What was that," Chris shouted as the men readied their weapons. Ake picked up his axe and groggily stood up.

"That, I think, was a weapon made to disorient me."

"You're damn right about that, youngling. With you out of the way, it would be easier to get the others. But since you are not dead, we'll just take you along with us."

The speaker was a man who had not covered his head. He had a face that was handsome in the way that hunters were handsome. His beard and moustache were very faint, as if he had recently started growing them. He had pointed ears, short hair, but his eyes ruined the entire figure. They were blood red, where the whites should have been. It looked as if his eyes had been made to bleed. As Ake looked closely at him, he noticed the strained but calm way in which the hunter spoke, as if he had all the time in the world. It was as if someone was speaking from behind him and he was just a carrier of the message.

Looking at his arms, Ake noticed a Black Raven tattoo that looked as if it was struggling to get out of his skin. Just then, he heard a roar and a figure dropped onto the rock.

Garon's father swung both his hunting knives at the people closest to him. His knives went through their robes and shattered their armour with an audible crunch. The hunter looked evidently afraid of the new figure who changed the entire equation of this fight. He hissed at Garon's father and said in a cold yet calm voice that portrayed no fear, "Hello Gregorz, long time no see, old friend."

"Our friendship ended when you betrayed me and left me on Bloodhound Mountain."

"I assumed you were dead. Also, I didn't want to leave you; I blacked out and next thing I knew, I was in the Capital, after being in a coma for five days. I was not even allowed to visit Logder to see you. This is the first I am seeing you after that incident. But come on, let bygones be bygones."

"Ok, in that case, you won't mind me doing this." So saying, Gregorz jumped at the hunter and three men charged to intercept him. They were thrown to the ground by Gregorz with inhuman speed. The hunter took out a broadsword. Pointing it at Garon's dad, he said, "I didn't want it to be this way, Gregorz. But if it has to be, it will be. You remember how good I was with a broadsword, don't you?"

"I do. And I also remember that I was the only one who could beat you. So, we are evenly matched."

Ake cast a risky glance below onto the ground where the three men had been thrown down. The contestants had evidently been taken to one of the tunnels, out of danger and seasoned warriors were standing in a loose ring around the rock. But what Ake could not understand was how Gregorz had managed to jump from the stands and land on the rock, which was almost in the centre of the stadium and a good one hundred and seventy metres away. As he watched the two closely, he noticed that the hunter was sweating, in spite of the cool climate of the stadium. He also noticed that his friend's dad had look of torment written across his face. Ake didn't know much about Garon's dad's past, but he didn't need to be an expert to figure out that Gregorz and the hunter had history.

As the two combatants eyed each other wearily, Ake noticed that they looked, almost, reluctant to use their weapons on each other. Garon's father he could understand, but not the other combatant. Killer with a conscience? Ake wondered to himself. Suddenly, the man with the red eyes lowered his sword and said, "I won't fight you. Kill me if you want, I am unguarded."

"No. Pick up your sword. I never fight a man or woman whose guard is down, you know that. Pick it up," Gregorz shouted, almost as if he was desperate for a fight.

"No," came the calm response.

"Pick it up!" Gregorz shouted as he lunged at the hunter with both his knives aimed at the calm hunter, forcing him to raise the broadsword to protect himself. The hunter looked like a puny guy in front of Gregorz; the former being only six feet three inches tall and his adversary was almost seven feet.

"I didn't want it to be this way, my friend. But, if it has to be like this, I will oblige you in a fight, a duel if you will."

Ake wondered how the speaker had such amount of patience and calm attitude. It also hadn't escaped his notice that the men had not attacked them in the time that Garon's dad and the hunter were trash talking.

"Yes." Gregorz sounded excited. "And I will kill you, sparing Lasgalan from the likes of you."

The two men jumped to the ground, where they immediately started duelling, knives on sword. The hunter's men also dropped and formed part of the circle of the duel. After a minute of fighting, they were not able to break each other's guard. Ake cast a glance at Garon, who had a look of worry across his face. The morning had turned from a friendly battle between Districts to a duel between titans. However, the warriors who had formed the loose ring around the rock didn't come in to assist in the duel, maintaining their positions. Two Taurians came on top of the rock to get the four boys to safety, but they refused to move.

Ake heard one of them say, "First time I've ever seen the Dark army's men refrain from subterfuges." As the fight progressed, Garon's dad started to get the upper hand and finally, after three minutes of fighting, broke the hunter's guard and the hunter hit the ground. As Gregorz came to him, the hunter smiled at him and said, "I know you won't do it. So, let me just say…. bye." He pushed himself back and, in a silver flash, he and his men were gone.

CHAPTER 17

Garon looked at his father as the latter looked as if his heart had been ripped out. He had never seen his father so unhinged that he wasn't even sure if his father was in the right frame of mind so that he could talk to him. He started to walk down the rock when he felt a hand on his shoulder. Turning, he saw Chris standing two feet from him. He said, "Did you know what happened between your dad and that man?" Garon shook his head and was about to say something when he heard the crowd fall silent. Looking at the gates, he saw five men walking out with eleven other contestants. As the man and his party came closer, Garon saw that Elesa was also there, looking as clueless as the other ten.

As the men came closer, Garon saw that they all wore suits of armour that had a Dragon on it. They motioned for the four youths to come down, which they did. Garon deduced that the men were Talons, and that something was about to happen. As they joined the group, one of the Talons spoke. "These fifteen youths have proven themselves to be a formidable force and we are here to take them to Talis." As he finished, the crowd roared in an incoherent voice. The Talon raised his hands to calm the crowd and continued, "We are taking them for reasons best known to us. I now make a small request to the relatives of these fifteen youths; please meet us in the field behind their buildings."

Turning towards the box, he addressed the figures there. "There will be no more continuation of the Games this year. The winner this year is no one. Let it be recorded in the archives." He turned to his comrades and said, "Bring them." Two of the men walked up the rock and jumped into the crowd, seeking out the relatives of the fifteen contestants. Meanwhile, the other two and their leader moved the contestants through the Horse tunnel, into their building and out into the field. Their parents, uncles and aunts were standing there. How they managed to get everyone so fast was a mystery to Garon, as the walk had taken them at least fifteen minutes. There were also another twenty Talons standing there. His dad went and stood with Hadran and Faldor, who said something to him to try and comfort him, most probably.

He was brought back to reality with a clap. One of the Talons was rubbing his palms together as if he had finally got the right cast for a play he wanted done.

"Alright, down to business. The fifteen of you are coming with us so that we can train you and prepare you for your destiny to become the most famous, fierce, and legendary warriors of Lasgalan. After all, that's what you were born to become. We start out in one week from here. You can't try and escape as the Taurians have tripled their security around this place. You will be furnished with everything that you need for this trip. Then, you will get a tour of the Empire that will be for two months. The rest will be told to you later. As for you, their parents," he faced the other group and continued. "You will have them for just this week. After that, you will see them only when you see them. That's the non-verbal promise you took when you decided to raise them as you own kids."

Garon looked at his parents, who were looking at him with sad eyes. He glanced at Faldor and Hadran, both of whom had straight faces, though Hadran's chin was trembling a bit.

Focusing his attention back on the Talon, Garon wondered if it was too late to say "You've got the wrong person here. I'm just a regular kid." Sadly, Garon knew that he was not his parents' biological kid, but that he was adopted. The Talon was still going through his monologue. "You fifteen are not chosen at random, but the choosing was done from before you were born. Each of you is different from each other as you have different skill-sets, different ways of dealing with threats. You come from different backgrounds, but there is more in common between you than you realise."

"Like having blonde hair and dark eyes," a question came from James.

"That is just an indicator that you are the ones Lasgalan will have Legends about," the Talon said. "But, yes, that is something you have in common," he continued.

Just then, one of the parents asked, "Where exactly are you going to be taking them?"

"These people are Talons. They will take the youngsters to their base in Talis, where they will be taken care of." Garon looked to see that the speaker was none other than Faldor.

The Talon nodded and said, "Any communication that concerns them will go through us. As you have seen today, there has been an attempt on their lives. There will continue to be until they fulfil their destiny and take their rightful place."

"And what is their destiny and rightful place," someone else asked.

"If I told you that, you would kill me," came the reply.

"If I entrust my child to you, what guarantee do I have that she will return in one piece, without a scratch?"

"I am a Talon. My honour is my word. But I can't say there won't be a scratch on them when they return."

Faldor stepped in and said, "Their security around the District walls is tight enough. Their cities have better defences than all the other cities of Lasgalan combined. I think that should suffice."

The Talon said, "Alright, one week. After that, the younglings are our responsibility. Do whatever you want with them, because after that we take over."

CHAPTER 18

C hris was allowed one week of absolute freedom to do what he wanted; something he was never allowed before. However, the one thing he was not allowed to do was to go to the other buildings; the Talons stopped him before he reached there. The one time he met his other friends was when they were out in the field, which the Talons allowed. He also met the third Raven from their District, a seventeen-year-old boy called Clint.

Clint used a peculiar weapon. At first glance, it looked like a spear. But on pressing a button near the base, the point shot out into three different heads, making it a trident. The tridents were weapons, which at one point, were considered an elite's weapon. Only skilled fighters used them in combat. A person needed strong arm muscles to wield a trident, and Clint certainly had them. Through the dawns and dusks of the week, Chris had seen him wield it with grace and elegance. Every time it opened up, there was no sound.

Now, Clint had a younger brother, Thomas. Thomas was the kind of guy people didn't mess around with, not once they saw his reed-like hands smack a rock into two pieces. He had a sense of humour that was very infectious and his jokes were so good that thinking about them could make somebody laugh. As the seventh day dawned, the boys got up and headed out to the front entrance of their buildings, where huge carriages awaited. As the luggage was being loaded, two Talons suddenly went and pulled out five more youths, one of them being Thomas. Their leader said, "They will be good for wielding the ultimate weapons."

Before Chris could comprehend what that meant, he was herded into the nearest carriage, where Garon and Clint were sitting, with their bags around them. Garon was reading a book whose title was "The old language of Lasgalan". Chris had no idea what interested Garon so much in a book, as Garon had already finished about thirty pages of the fat book. As Chris climbed into the carriage and placed his bags down, Clint turned to him and said, "'Morning, Chris. Beautiful day isn't it?"

"Yeah, sure is," Garon muttered. Clearly, he resented being separated from his family. He glared at the back of one of the Talons who was separating the others into groups. Chris sensed that Garon was a bit angry, but tried to reason it out. "It may be for the best, Garon. Who knows what's out there, waiting for us to probably make a decision that could alter their lives? We don't, and that is the beautiful part."

Garon looked up, and Chris saw that his words made a bit of sense to Garon. The anger in the Wolf's eyes subsided a bit, but still looked angry. He got back to reading the book while Clint asked Chris, "How'd you sleep, knowing that this was the day you would be separated from your parents for some time?"

"Well, I just made the most of my time, Clint. You know that Thomas is also coming with us?"

"Seriously? Man, this will be a fun trip."

"Don't get too excited, Raven. He's in another carriage and only three people per carriage," came the Talon leader's voice as he rounded the carriage. "It's about a three-day travel to Talis so you have plenty of time to meet him. Now, let's get a move on." He pulled up a wooden plank to stop anything from falling out from the back during the journey and proceeded to do the same with the other carriages. He and some others then walked to the centre of the ring of carriages and, in a silver flash, disappeared. The rest of the Talons got onto the carriages or their Horses and their little group moved out of the city, into the morning.

As they left the city limits, Chris saw the carriage driver pull a hood onto his head, as if he didn't want to be spotted. Chris looked back and saw that the other drivers had done the same. He was about to ask their driver why they did so, but thought the better of it. He started talking to Clint about life at his end of the District, Clint living near the mountains on the east and Chris living on the west coast. From time to time, Clint would glance at Garon as if he was afraid that the boy reading the book would suddenly go berserk and kill everyone in close vicinity.

As the sun progressed to its midday position, the driver started talking with them, and soon even Garon lost interest in his book and got into the conversation. They spoke as if they were old friends who met after a long time. There were laughs and jokes around, but Luca, their driver, was the best at cracking jokes.

"Now listen up guys," he said. "We will be passing the Jet-Horn pass soon. At this pace, we should be there by tomorrow morning. We pass through it into Covis and then north into Talis. We won't stop till evening when we break for an hour and then on again till nightfall. If you get hungry, there is chicken and eggs in the yellow boxes. Help yourselves to them."

The trio opened the boxes and just as Clint was about to eat an egg, there was a sound of an explosion. Chris shot his hand into his bag and took out his mace, Clint his spear and Garon his daggers. Luca took their Horses off the road into a clump of bushes and in seconds, the other carriages had done the same. Luca motioned for the passengers to stay out of sight as he drew out knuckledusters with some claws on them. He peered out of the bushes and from what Chris could see, there were just bulls roaming through the trees on the other side of the road; they had sought shelter for no reason, but the explosive sound made it seem as if they were under attack. The drivers returned to the carts and they were on the road again. Luca suddenly asked Garon, "What ability do you possess?"

"Well, I can throw a dagger very accurately if that's what you're looking for."

"No, no. I mean what is your bodily enhancement that makes you different from everyone except the other fifteen of our group?"

"I don't know."

"Ok. What about you, Chris?"

Chris responded saying, "When I find out, I will let you know."

"And before you ask me, Luca, I will tell you mine," Clint said. "I can assess any threat and find useful ways to subdue it and I have a problem with authority. I also wield a mean weapon, so don't try and command me all the time because I might accidently kill you."

"Hmm. We will see about that. I have to train the three of you when we reach Talis, so no fooling around. And Chris, I will find out about your abilities before you can tell me. Got it?" The last two sentences were said in a serious tone, but there was some humour the way Luca said it. They got back to eating and soon Clint went off to sleep and Garon was reading his book so intensely that it took five calls of his name for him to look up at Chris.

Chris asked Garon, "Want to play a game?"

"Sure. What game?"

So, for the next fifteen minutes, Chris taught Garon a card game that was unique to only Covis. They spent the next two hours playing that, Chris winning every nine out of ten games. Garon asked him at one point, "How do you win like this?"

"Actually, it takes a minute to learn. But it takes a lifetime to master. There are old men and women in Covis who have played it from childhood, but we youngsters can beat them from time to time. It's more a game of logic and being able to see your opponent's moves, at least four moves before he or she makes them."

"You boys better be able to predict battle situations as they progress. One of the lessons in your training in Talis will be based on that. You will have to fight for your life."

"You don't like to take chances," realised Garon. "Why?"

"The Talons have spent the last two centuries in search of the Ones who would bring down Yedgal. Whenever we thought we found them and tried to train them in their own Districts, Yedgal's men would hunt them down within a month, and some of us were fortunate not to be there at that time. I don't suppose you know this, but your father was also one of them. He is the only one alive from his generation of Chosen Ones. So, we are taking all of you to Talis, where our full force might hold out against his men and give you guys a chance of survival."

"Are you saying that Yedgal was more than two hundred years when King Rendaf's father killed him," Chris asked.

"He was considered immortal and invincible up till then. There was no injury from which he could not heal, no man that could best him in anything. Finally, with the help of a powerful weapon and more than three-fourths of the Talon force, King Rendaf's father killed the tyrant, right in his throne."

"Which District did Yedgal hail from?"

"No one knows for sure. There is no record of him anywhere, and trust me, we searched records dating back three hundred years and came up with nothing." There was a hint of anger in Luca's voice but he hid it well. Chris started feeling sleepy and went to sleep as soon as he put his head down. The next thing he knew, Garon was shaking him awake. They had arrived at a clearing which was about hundred metres across. The other carriages had done the same. It was around evening time, as Luca had promised. The trio got out and went to meet their friends. Chris went to meet James and found him talking to Ake and laughing away with their carriage driver.

As James saw Chris coming towards them, he excused himself and went to him.

"How was your ride, James?"

"Oh, pretty good actually. My driver, Reidan, he is actually a funny guy. He said that he would be training me himself in Talis."

"My driver said the same thing. He said he would be training Clint, Garon and myself. His name is Luca."

Chris realised that James was not as rough-around-the-edges as he normally was with new people. He glanced around to a carriage where Ake was talking to a girl. Pointing his chin at them, he asked, "Who is Ake talking to?"

"Oh, that's his sister, Hasha."

"She's cute."

James looked at Chris and asked, "Are you mad? Ake has…" He was about to say something else when Ake's voice came from behind him.

"Ok, who called my sister cute? It was one of you two, so 'fess up. Now."

James whirled around to see Ake standing behind them, axe in hand. He tried for a smile and said, "Ake, no one said anything. You probably…"

"Don't try and con me James. I don't like liars very much, especially if they are my friends. So, who said it?" The grip on the double-bladed axe became a bit harder.

"Ok Ake. It was me," Chris said.

Ake looked at him and, pointing the axe at him, said, "Never do that again." He walked back to the carriage to his sister and once James felt he was out of earshot, he told Chris, "Don't worry. He's fourteen. He will probably forget about this by tomorrow."

"I don't think so. That one sentence sounded deadly. He looked like he was ready to fillet me like a fish."

Chris looked over at Garon who was talking to another girl who was also a Wolf. Like everyone else, the trio in Luca's carriage was given arm-guards that went from their wrist to their elbow. The youngsters were given arm-guards marked with the animal of their District. Somehow, the drivers knew which species of animal was the respective youngster's as Chris was given one of a Mountain Raven, Clint that of a Black Raven, and James also had one of a Mountain Raven. Chris recalled Luca giving Garon one with a Wolf's; Luca saying it was an Ag-Wolf.

As the duo of Ravens talked, the drivers went into the trees and were not seen until the end of the hour. Soon they were back on the road, heading into the sunset. Garon became quite inquisitive in this period and asked Luca a lot of questions, Luca answering them without betraying any sign of impatience. Once it became dark, four torches, located at the corners of the carriages alit on their own. They gave off an orange flame, but no smoke. A question was asked about that as well, the answer being that it was enchanted wood. Looking back at the other carriages, Chris wondered what their youngsters were doing. He was about to lie down when Luca said, "Once we stop for the night, you guys sleep. Don't try and sleep now."

It was another hour before they came to a smaller clearing than the other, about fifty metres across. The drivers arranged the carriages in a circle and disembarked. They came back in five minutes, and seeing everyone mixed up, ordered them back inside the carriages. Luca handed them blankets that were very warm and told them to go to sleep. The last thing Chris saw before he shut his eyes was one of the drivers throw something in the ground and a green light shooting upwards and bursting in all directions.

CHAPTER 19

Clint woke up suddenly in the night. Thanks to his father, who was an astronomer, he could tell what time in the night it was. And it was just about three hours to dawn. He needed to take a leak, so he silently got off the carriage, headed to the nearest tree and waited to finish his job. As he headed back, he noticed that he was not the only one awake. Luca, too, was awake and a little away from the group. As Clint approached him, Luca softly asked, without turning to him, "Couldn't sleep?"

"No. I needed to take a leak. And then I saw you were here as well, so…"

"Hmm. I suppose it is in human nature to be a bit curious about something you may not understand at that point in time."

"You're good with words, I must say."

"Ha. I'm actually here on guard duty for another hour. Then someone else will take over till dawn and we will be on our way. We don't expect an attack, but as Garon said, we don't like taking chances."

"What was that green thing you shot into the sky? Some kind of defensive charm?"

"Yes. We at Talis must know how to use every single weapon made in Lasgalan. That makes us very tough to fight no matter what weapon we have. I saw your weapon. Who gave it to you?"

"My grandfather, on his deathbed. He gave it to me on my fourteenth birthday and said it would keep me safe as long as I wielded it. I wish he was still alive. He was a good person to confide in. He kept my secrets and he kept Thomas'. He is the one who got me my Raven when I was born."

"The way you speak of him, it seems you loved him a lot." Taking in a long breath Luca said, "I wish I knew what it was like to have a family."

"What do you mean?"

"My family was killed by Yedgal himself when I was just a boy. He did that in front of me. I was young, but young enough to remember. Every time I go to sleep, I see their faces. Yedgal burnt our house and left me for dead. The Talons found me in the ruins and raised me as their own. I was told later that I was also a Chosen One. But that was after Yedgal was dead. There were only five Chosen Ones alive when Yedgal died. Rendaf's father was one of them, for some reason. He was about fifty years old."

"You're an easy person to talk to, I must say."

"Aren't you feeling a bit sleepy?"

"No. Besides, I'll keep you company till your shift ends."

"I appreciate that, but I'd rather you go to sleep now." Before Clint could say anything, Luca pressed his palm against his forehead and Clint felt waves of sleep crash over him. He reached the carriage and immediately went to sleep.

Three hours later, Clint woke up and shook Chris awake. Garon was already up and reading his book. Chris asked him, "Do you plan on finishing that book before we reach Talis?"

"Well, it's the first volume in a five-book collection. So yeah, maybe I will finish it."

The carriage went on west. Clint and Luca had an intense conversation about the importance of games in life. Clint was for the cause. At one point, he said that if he was king of Lasgalan, he would institute a system of games every four years. For some reason, Luca smiled and said, "When you're king, a simple decision like that can be very complicated." Clint looked into the distance and wondered what was waiting for him in Talis. He thought about his family heading back home. He was thankful that even Thomas was accompanying him, otherwise he would have felt lonely. What he did not know was that Chris looked up to him. Back in Covis, Clint was like a Legend. Covis wasn't as big as the other Districts, but it was the most advanced in most areas. Army, small in number, but it had firepower and weaponry that rivalled the other Districts. Economy, much better than Logder and Tauris, despite the fact that Tauris got heavy income due to the annual Games. Literacy, a hundred percent. Then came the others at ninety-four to ninety-five percent. Covis had produced most of the winners of the Games in the last fifty years. They maintained friendly relations with all the Districts and never got into war with them. Clint recruited himself into the army the year before and was already famous throughout the District as the boy with no conscience as he apparently killed without a second thought.

As the carriage turned a bend in the road, there was a gold flash in front of them, and a man walked out of the flash. He looked familiar, but Clint couldn't place him, though a memory of him was a recent one. He heard Garon speak in shock, "This joker again? He must be crazy to take us on alone."

"Well, too many cooks spoil the broth, don't they?" The man said.

That's when Clint remembered where he saw the man. He was the same one who had halted the Games and caused him to run to a tunnel, and Clint wasn't the cowardly type.

Clint took out his weapon, which was no more than a foot long. The man laughed and said, "Are you going to fight me with a stick?" Clint gave no answer, but jumped down and sliced the stick down. Instantly, there was a spear in his hand, about as tall as the wielder. The man's eyes betrayed a little fear at the sight of the weapon. Clint pointed it at him and said, "Leave now, or face my wrath." One year in the army had taught him not to fight unless he was attacked first.

"What wrath? You do not have a grievance against me. I just need to take back two of you. Anyone will do. The boss isn't picky."

"You and your boss can go to the Underworld for all I care," came Luca's voice, now next to Clint. Clint realised that the man was going easy on time; he wasn't worried about delays. However, before any of them could move a muscle, the man's red whites changed to regular whites and in a big effort addressed Luca, "Get them to Talis fast. I can only hold him out for about a minute. Go!"

In a gold flash, the man disappeared. Luca and Clint got back in the carriage and they were on their way again. Clint saw that they were moving faster than normal and thought about the man they had encountered. It seemed that he had schizophrenia. He noticed that they were entering a hilly area and said, "We are heading into Jet-Horn, aren't we?"

"Yes, we are. Keep your voices down. A small sound can cause a landslide here."

For the next hour, the trio spoke to each other in sign language. It was easy, considering that they were taught it in their youth. There were no jokes and the hour was also tension-filled as there were frequent crashes of trees and caws of Ravens that could have sent the parade underground. Once they emerged on the other side, Clint drew in a breath to compensate for the breath taken away by the view. Luca laughed and said, "Welcome to Covis, guys. About three hundred feet below us is the source of the Jet River, Covis' main river."

"And just north of here is my hometown." Clint's eyes watered up. He'd been away from his home for nearly six months and just being near it was enough to make him feel like a small kid.

"I'm sorry, but we can't stop here, Clint. We need to reach the training centre by evening."

"Look, from here to Talis is an open run; almost flat land. My house comes on the way. Give me fifteen minutes and you won't regret it."

"Fine. You have fifteen minutes, no more."

The carriages went on and soon they were on the outskirts of a city. Clint anxiously awaited seeing his house. Upon seeing it, he went inside to his parent's room, only to see his father sitting there, looking as if his world was taken apart.

Clint shook his shoulders and said, "Dad, why are you so sad? I am back. Where's mum?"

His dad looked into his eyes, and Clint understood what happened. He was too shocked to stand and collapsed into his favourite chair, his head spinning with questions. Shaking himself a bit out of his shock, he asked, "How?"

His father spoke in an almost inaudible voice, "Yedgal."

Clint nearly screamed. He steeled himself and thought about the last time he spoke to his mother. He felt so angry that he started to feel pain in his shoulder blades, as if something was trying to get out. He looked in his father's eyes, which were full of revenge.

"My son, when you find him, don't hesitate. Kill him, and send him to the Underworld."

Clint nodded. "No one will get in my way. If they do, they'll be at the receiving end of the trident."

"Go now. Remember, your mother is always with us, in here," Clint's father placed his hand on Clint's heart. "Go now. Avenge her."

"Goodbye, dad."

Clint walked out and headed to the carriage. As he set foot inside, Garon said, "What happened?"

"My mom has passed on. Please don't ask me anything else."

Chris, in a startled voice asked, "What's on your back?"

"Nothing," Clint snapped. "My mom was killed by Yedgal. When I see him, I am going to do such things to him, that he will wish he never killed her."

"No, I'm serious. Something red is protruding out of your shoulder blades."

"He's right. It's like you're bleeding." Garon pulled Clint's shirt off and whatever he saw clearly shocked him. "By

Lasgalan." He touched whatever it was, and sent shivers along Clint's spine. They guided his hands to something light yet rough. Luca also saw it and exclaimed, "Garon, tell all the others to pick up the pace."

They were supposed to stop for a mid-morning break, but Luca wouldn't hear of it. According to him, Clint's condition was more important than anything at that point. They were going too fast to even drink water without spilling some. Clint still wondered what had shocked the other three so much that they were going at three times the regular speed. Soon, they were in Talis and heading to a city that was maybe another hour away. Luca was saying something under his breath that Clint could not understand, but the tone was one of urgency.

As they reached the city walls, twenty-foot doors opened for them and shut as soon as the last one was in. Luca addressed the entire group, "This is just a stop for a half-hour. We will leave again, so do whatever you want."

Garon and Chris took one last glance at Clint, who waved them away. He walked into a shop and asked the shopkeeper for two mirrors. He went into a private room and angled the mirrors so that he could see his back.

Garon was right. He had been bleeding, though they had stopped that. Across the length of his shoulder blades, the skin had parted to make way for something white and red. His veins were visible as thin red lines around the area. He touched it, and came to the conclusion that these things were the light and rough things he had felt earlier.

He came out of the room and handed the mirrors back. He came out into the area where the carriages were. He went straight to Luca, who was talking to another driver. Luca came and asked him, "Did you see what it was?"

"Yes. What is this?"

"You are not a regular human; you already know that. But you are more unique than the others, as you are embodied with the spirit of your Tribe, an eagle. These things on your back, my friend, are the beginning of your wings."

Clint wasn't sure that heard him correctly. "Wings?"

"Yes, wings. Every District's Tribes have someone every hundred years, who is embodied by their respective Tribe's spirit. Covis'…"

"Wait, you mean to say that I was born from the Eagle Tribe of Covis?"

"All of you are born of the Tribes. You were sent away due to the danger Yedgal's men posed. They could not allow anyone to oppose their master's rise to power again. The only Tribe to face complete annihilation was Logder's Wolf Tribe. Yedgal's men killed them off about thirteen years ago. After that, the other Tribes of Lasgalan began contesting to have more influence over Rendaf. The Wolves were able to keep them in line. But now, the situation in the courts of Lasgalan are bad. There is no one to advise Lord Huy and he just about keeps things in line in Logder. For how much longer is the question."

"You mean the other Tribes are alive, somewhere?"

"Yes. They are in hiding. Even we can't find them. Every month, a representative from the Tribes visits Rendaf, advises him and leaves. They don't see eye to eye on everything, but keep the safety of Lasgalan as their top priority. But enough of talk, let's get you back into the carriage. We got another hour's journey to cover before we reach our destination."

Clint started to take a step, but he felt something in his back snap. He crumpled to his knees and let out a loud scream.

Within seconds, Garon and Chris were next to him, taking him on their shoulders and as they headed to the carriage, Clint saw the others watching him with uneasy expressions. The duo placed him on the floor of their ride, but Luca said, "Keep him upright. The doctors need to see him without further injuries." Clint was in a lot of pain, and his army training was not enough to help bear the pain. For the better part of the hour, he slept, which helped decrease the pain somewhat. But once he was up, it came back, almost with a vengeance. He had already regurgitated twice and didn't feel too good. Finally, Luca said the words, "We're almost there."

Clint glanced in front and saw they were on a small bridge over a river heading into a small town. In front of them was a small road that rounded the corner on what looked the tallest building of the locality. As they came down, Luca took a different route than the others and came to the largest building. He pointed at Clint and told the Talons in front of him.

"His back is in a bad condition. Give him an intensive treatment and send him back." Three people got him down and kept his bags in the carriage. He was taken into the building, which he figured was a hospital. He was put face-down onto a bed and the doctor pulled his shirt up. The doctor gave Clint some water to drink before he could do anything. Clint drank it in seconds and crashed on the bed, sinking into a dreamless sleep.

CHAPTER 20

Dan had seen a lot of strange things over the last month. He had seen a man walk into a raging fire to rescue a baby and come out unscathed. He had seen a young boy with reed-like arms break a rock without showing any pain. But what he did not expect was an army-trained boy of seventeen to sprout wings. He had seen Clint walk into a shop, blood over the back of his shirt and decided to follow him. He went into the room next to Clint's and waited to see what the problem was. There was a small gap in the wall between the two rooms and he saw the reflection of the white wings sprouting from Clint's shoulder blades. He waited for Clint to get out of the room, waited for a minute and got out of the shop. He didn't tell anyone about it, but waited to get a move on again. However, when Clint was brought to his knees five minutes later, clutching his back, Dan knew what the cause was.

He waited patiently to get to the Talons' base for his training. His two companions, Ake and Emmanuel, were good conversationalists and Dan had great fun talking with them. He was sleeping when the group reached their destination. On waking up, he gathered whatever of his stuff was loose and stowed them in his bag. Apart from Clint's carriage the others took a right from the bridge and came to a dead end between two buildings. Lumenta, their driver and Trainer, told them to disembark and go into the building, where they would be guided to their room. The other teenagers also followed and were put into separate rooms. Dan put his stuff on a bed and went outside to the balcony. He was joined by Ake who said, "Now, we have about four hours to sunset. What are we supposed to do?"

"Well, I will tell you your schedule first." Lumenta's voice came from behind them.

The two of them turned around to see their Trainer standing at the doorway. Lumenta continued, "You guys may or may not be interacting with your friends most of the day, but you may encounter them during your training sessions. Now, breakfast will be at sunrise. You will eat with everyone else. One hour there. Next, you will bathe. Another hour there. After that you have to come to a room in this building for three hours to learn about yourselves and your advancements. Then you have an hour's break for lunch with everybody else. You then will be taken to a room for daily assessment by our health specialists. After that is a half-hour break and you will come down to the training field, which I will show you later. After we finish, whenever that is, you will be allowed to visit your other friends till evening. Then, all of you can go to another playing field we have to play any sport of your choice. Once you are done with your learning, you will be taught about different weapons, but you will have to use your preferred weapon in training." Luca turned and walked to the door. Dan suddenly asked, "What happened to Clint?"

"Oh, I was just going to check on that myself. Stay in your room for now please. We will call you down in a bit." Dan went back to the balcony, alone this time and surveyed the view. Looking left, he saw others had also come out of their rooms to check out the view. He saw a small but long building beyond the residential buildings and looking at the covered plates going in, guessed it was the dining room. There was a gentle wind that was blowing from the river. It was such a peaceful place that Dan didn't mind staying the rest of his life here. He went to his bed and proceeded to unpack his stuff. The bath was adjoining the room, not a common one with another room. He took his armour out and put it on the hook on the wall next to his bed. The others proceeded to do the same. Soon they had arranged their stuff and sat around chatting. Dan thought of something and asked his roommates, "Do you think this is a trap?"

Emmanuel was the first to respond, "It could be, but we can't jump to conclusions like that. Even if it is a trap, don't you think we would have been told what a wonderful place this is?"

"True that. But they didn't need to say that; the atmosphere of this place is doing that for them. That's why I'm asking."

The trio decided to explore the place a bit, so they got out of the room and headed down the corridor, past others' rooms, where the occupants were either crashed out or talking amongst themselves. Dan saw that Clint's carriage friends were sitting on their beds, one reading a book that was almost over, and the other was polishing his mace. The duo gave no indication of seeing the trio. As they got back on the streets, Ake said, "Let's go to the river. We'll be able to get to places faster."

They headed to the riverbank that was overlooked by their balcony. It was fenced up, but there were stairs leading to a lower level, almost at the surface of the river. It was a nice secluded spot, where the balconies couldn't get a view of them. Dan had always heard of fast rivers, but the river in front of him was really fast. He saw a feather whiz past him so fast, it took him a second to realise it had passed him. They were skipping stones on the surface when they heard someone talking above them.

"...telling you, he is lucky to be alive. The growth is at regular pace, but it should have started at least six months back to reach its current position. The only other explanation is that..."

The voices moved away from them, but Ake and Emmanuel looked intrigued enough to follow them to see what they were talking about. Sadly, Dan felt sure he knew what growth was being discussed. They stayed near the water's edge until they got bored and walked around the small town. They finished their journey in an hour and went back to their room. Coming back, Dan went inside for a bath and the others followed suit. They waited for Lumenta to come back and were already getting restless.

Lumenta came to the room later and faced the boys. "You already saw the place, didn't you?"

The trio nodded.

"Can't blame you for being restless. Anyway, Dan, Clint is alright. He will have to be taken care of for another day, though. You guys have got this evening to be with your friends. Tomorrow, training starts."

After Lumenta left, Dan locked the door and asked the others if they were interested in playing sports later. They immediately changed into their sports clothes while cracking jokes on each other's weapon of choice. They were ready in ten minutes and Dan grabbed his volleyball from the bag.

"Knew I was right to bring something of entertainment."

Ake and Emmanuel rolled their eyes in a sarcastic manner and they headed out after loafing around in the room. The doors they passed were all shut, which meant that the occupants were either sleeping or they wanted privacy. The playing field was near the dining room. It was convenient because after a day of hard exercise, the youths would want to eat as fast as possible and then go to sleep. There were two volleyball courts, one football field and one basketball court. The boys were soon taking shots across the net, the latter being tall even for Emmanuel, who was six and a half feet tall. Then again, Dan had seen that the shortest person in their group was only six feet tall, one of them being himself. Dan thought he was good in volleyball, having played for Equis' volleyball team for two years, but Emmanuel was excellent. He had to jump to get the ball over the net, granted, but even with two of them hitting the ball hard, he didn't break a sweat getting it from one end of the court to the other. He was a natural at volleyball, but claimed he had never touched the ball in his life. Soon, a group of girls came down to the courts, two of them Equines and the other being a Wolf. The third girl, he learned, was Ake's sister, Hasha.

The girls and boys played a friendly three-on-three match, which the boys won by a close margin. The girls were called back inside by their Trainer, Vulca, who looked as if she could put down the three boys without any effort. Dan made a mental note not to get into any arguments with the Trainers, because they all looked like Vulca and were probably part-time professional wrestlers. The boys got back to playing volleyball and nearly shot the ball out of the field a few times. One thing that was missing was the company of the others. Then, almost in one group, they came out. Soon, Dan saw, all three sports were being played and the Trainers were also out. Something struck Dan and he went to Lumenta.

"I have a question to ask, if you don't mind."

"Shoot."

"How did you guys know when to start searching for us?"

Before answering, Lumenta shouted in an impossibly loud voice, "Everybody gather around." When everyone was assembled, he said, "Edward, Victoria, Trest, step forward please."

Two girls and a boy stepped out of the group. The boy was about seventeen and the girls were sixteen and fifteen. Lumenta continued, "When we found out about them, we knew that we had to start searching for you. You three, show your powers."

Edward closed his eyes in concentration and the air around him heated up fast. He burst into flames and the ones closest to him backed up quickly.

The elder girl, Victoria, did nothing but stared directly into Dan's eyes and it was as if she was sending a message to him. He started feeling sleepy, but Lumenta stopped her and asked her to wake him up. Suddenly, Dan felt more awake than he had ever been.

"Vibes," Dan said. "You use vibes to get people to do things."

Victoria smiled shyly and looked at the ground.

The youngest girl, Trest, whipped out a knife that looked sharp enough to slice through armour. She cut her arm down her centre vein, and blood flowed out slowly. As they watched, the bleeding slowed down, and her skin healed, not revealing that she had cut it just before.

Vulca stepped in and said, "Ok. All of you sit down and tell us about yourselves."

All twenty-two of them sat on the stone benches in accordance to their District, four on each of the six benches, with the exception of Covis as Clint was not there, and Talis where someone was missing. Dan went first.

"Hello. I'm Dan, from Equis. I am a good archer and also a berserker. I can fire any arrow from any bow, and I can sense the emotions of humans and animals. I am not a psychologist, so don't expect me to help you deranged people."

There were a few laughs, and Dan felt Victoria's shyness going down a bit.

After him was Robert. Robert was an excellent wrestler, and never showed emotion except every now and then. Even Dan couldn't get a good read on his emotions. Then was Isabella, who could sense where traps were hidden. She claimed she could dismantle one or make one from scratch. Then was Isabella's elder sister, Adriana. She didn't have a power, but was a good orator.

Then came the Ravens. Chris went first. His weapon was a solid mace. Before he said what his power was, he looked at his Trainer and said, "Sorry I didn't tell you before, but I can change any body structure of mine at will." To prove his point, he concentrated and his height increased slightly. His arms became thicker and his voice changed to that of a girl. More laughs followed the voice. James was good with knives and said that he didn't know his power. At that, his Trainer said, "You can turn invisible at will, and are quite elusive." Then was Clint's younger brother, Thomas. He said he could break a rock into two, which everyone had seen in Tauris. He said that Clint was a good trident fighter, and that Clint had a problem with authority. How he got into the army, Thomas had no idea.

The Bulls went after the Ravens. There was Gonth, who could wield a sword and shield. He claimed that, if he had the details of all opposing sides of a battle, he could predict the outcome of the battle before it started. Emmanuel was next. His weapon was a club. He said that if a challenge was issued at him, he wouldn't back down from it. After him was Karen.

Karen's weapon was a scythe, which she said was good for torturing people. Her elder brother, Adrian was last, and he said that he was good at spying.

Next were the Lions. Jacob went first. He was a very intimidative person, and as if that was not enough, his weapons were knuckledusters made of pure iron. His successor was Vincent, who could hit any target accurately within half a league. His preferred weapon was a javelin. Then was Anne. She was an expert at breaking and entering, so she claimed. She relied on brute strength, and said that she only had to look at something once and could memorise it. She could look at a map and have all its features committed to memory. She could draw a map of any place with every feature accurate. The last Lion was Patrick. He was a guy who leapt before he looked. He was Vincent's younger brother.

The Wolves were the last. Ake went as the first one. His weapon was a double-bladed axe and his power was his sharp hearing. Next was Garon, Clint's carriage mate. He used daggers and claimed that his eyes were more powerful than others. They could see through objects and see in darkness like a snake. Then, only two girls were left. Elesa wielded a sword and relied on uncontrolled rage to help her in battle. She was not a berserker, though. The last speaker of the session was Hasha, Ake's elder sister. She was not good in battle, but was a good runner.

After they finished, Vulca and Lumenta called out to a girl named Vesper, who was Edward's cousin. She went with them into the dining room and went back to her room later on. The group went back to their sports and were soon called inside for dinner. The sun had set long ago, but the torches placed around the field provided sufficient light to play.

As they trooped into the hall, they saw Clint sitting and eating his dinner. Garon and Chris went to him and sat next to him for the rest of the meal. They had to sit in according to their training groups, so Ake, Dan and Emmanuel sat together. There was a lot of meat on the table, ranging from chicken, duck, eggs, ham, bacon, veal, venison, beef and mutton. There were vegetables as well, in the same quantity as the meats. Soon, everyone was chowing down and there was some chatter around the place. As they were on their desserts, James' Trainer stood up and announced, "Tomorrow, you sorry lot will be getting something that will protect you in even the most dire of dire straits. As for what it is, you will see tomorrow." He sat down, and the chatter increased in volume. As Dan finished, he told Ake he was going up and left. He hadn't got the hang of the roads and asked around for directions to their building. As he climbed the steps, he got the feeling that someone was following him. Pretending he knew nothing, he went to the room, quickly taking out an arrow from his quiver that he kept out for emergencies, and hid behind the door. Someone opened the door and Dan shot out from behind it, the arrowhead two inches from the stalker's throat.

"Really," Victoria asked. "This is how you greet a friend?"

CHAPTER 21

Victoria stared calmly at Dan. He put the arrow down and asked, "What do you want?"

"Well, you want to sense my emotions or do you want me to spell it out for you?"

Dan sighed; he wasn't going to get a straight answer. He sensed the vibes Victoria was giving off, and he didn't like what he saw. "Get out of my room before I call a Trainer," he warned Victoria.

"Now, why would you do that?" Victoria didn't seem to be afraid of him, though Dan couldn't understand why. He stared down Victoria, until Victoria sighed and turned to the door and walked out saying, "Boys." Dan stood rooted to his place for a minute before he remembered to move. He put his arrow back in the quiver and went inside the bathroom to change. When he came out, Ake and Emmanuel were waiting for him. They also changed and soon, the trio were talking with Chris and Garon. They said that Clint was out of danger of fatal damage, but would have to stay at the hospital through the night. They hoped that he would be making an appearance the next day. There was a lot of laughter along their corridor.

Chris stared out of the door leading to the balcony and said, "You know, we only occupy this level of the building, the others are taken over by the Trainers."

Emmanuel asked, "What about the girls?"

"They are in the other building, also with their Trainers."

"How do you know that?"

Chris smiled mysteriously and said, "I have my sources."

Just then, Luca came and said, "Chris, Garon. You have five minutes before you go back to the room for the night." The duo nodded affirmation and went back to their room. Dan felt as if there was something amiss in the room. On a hunch, he went on all fours and looked under the beds. Under Emmanuel's was a small bottle, capped and containing green liquid. Dan shouted for Lumenta, not touching the bottle. Lumenta came into the room, took stock of the situation, and ordered Dan to chuck the bottle into the river below. Dan threw it into the river and waited for an explosion to occur, but Lumenta assured him that the river would render the liquid useless and there would be no explosion. They waited for two minutes before Lumenta told them to get into bed. As Lumenta was about to shut the door, Ake said, "Lumenta, I need to tell you something." He went to their Trainer and exchanged a few words with him. Lumenta put his hand on his shoulder and told him some reassuring words. Ake came back into the room. Climbing into bed, he pointed a finger at Dan and said, "Don't even think about it."

"Think about what, Ake?"

"Sensing his emotion," Emmanuel said.

"I wasn't planning on it, but since you value your privacy, I won't." Dan assured them. As he was the last one in bed, the torches on the walls of their room went out with him. As he went out, he could almost feel Ake giving out guilty emotions, though he wasn't sure why.

CHAPTER 22

Dan woke up at the crack of dawn, with the room filled with faint sunlight. Looking at his friends, who were still sleeping, he went and washed his face. He wasn't a good sleeper, but last night's sleep was unlike any other he ever had. No dreams, no back stiffness like he normally experienced when he woke up. They had about a half-hour before sunrise, so he figured that he better make the most of it. He went to the balcony, not making a sound, and stared out across the river. In the faint, fast-fading moonlight, he could see just a bit to the opposite bank.

He looked back at his sleeping friends, and reluctantly opened his senses to embrace his friends' emotions. He didn't have a good range, but he got back a lot of good emotion. There were twenty-three, which meant that Clint was in his room. He was about to close his senses, when he felt another set of emotions, this one not human. He tried to shut his senses, but more came in. In addition to his friends', he now had another eighteen emotions, all of them non-human. He shut his eyes tight and concentrated hard. He had never tried to hold so many emotions simultaneously, and gripped the railing so tightly, he thought his knuckles had gone white. He felt a hand on his shoulder and the emotions shut down, leaving his mind clear. He opened his eyes, turned around, and saw Ake and Emmanuel standing on either side of him, making the balcony a tight squeeze.

Dan let go of the railing and said, "Sorry, guys. I just thought…"

Before he could go on, Emmanuel said, "It is alright, Dan. Sometimes you need to run before you can walk. At least now you know what will happen if you try to run too fast."

Dan smiled weakly and said, "Fine. Wash up. Breakfast is in a half hour."

Soon, they were walking down to the dining room and watching the mist curl off the field and courts. Dan walked in first and saw that their breakfast was a high-protein one. There was meat on the table, though not as much as the previous night. They sat down and the others started pouring in. They were done in about forty-five minutes and went back to their respective rooms. Since they had more than enough time to get ready, they finished bathing and stayed in their room till they were summoned. The placard on their door read "Lumenta". All the boys were heading to rooms on the bottom floor. They were separated into their groups. The room was of considerable size, and Lumenta was waiting for them.

As they took their seats, Lumenta started, "Right, let's start. Any questions you want to ask me before we start?"

No one said anything.

"Ok. As you know, you are not regular humans. You are actually born of your respective District's Tribes. Now a little into Lasgalan. There are six Districts, but only five Tribes. The Wolf Tribe was annihilated by Yedgal's men and as a result, no one survived. They were surprised in the night thirteen years ago and after that, the other Tribes went into hiding. After that, the other Tribes of Lasgalan began contesting to have more influence over Rendaf. The Wolves were able to keep them in line. But now, the situation in the courts of Lasgalan are bad. There is no one to advise Lord Huy and he just about keeps things in line in Logder. For how much longer is the question. We call it the 'War of the Tribes'."

"Can we skip the history lesson, Lumenta?" Ake popped a question. Lumenta smiled and said, "Ok. Onto you then. Now I will explain everything about yourselves, from the inside to out. Co-operate with me, and we can get this done today and from tomorrow, we can get down to your formal training."

The boys nodded.

"Good. First things first. You must be wondering why you are tall for your age. The answer is simple. Gravity doesn't have as strong a hold on you as it would on a regular human. You emit your own gravitational field. That opposes some of the gravity acting on you and as a result, you are taller. Your gravity is weak compared to Lasgalan's but it is considerable. Any questions till here?"

The trio shook their heads.

"The next part is your skeleton. Humans have a calcium-based skeleton, but you guys have a calcium-based skeleton with a thin coating of iron on it. This helps you withstand impacts from heavy objects like rocks and boulders. You can be cut along the flesh though. Any blade hitting your bone will shatter on impact. Don't think you are invulnerable."

Emmanuel asked, "Is there any way in which we could die in battle?"

"Oh, yes. There are a few. Decapitation, acid burning, ripping out your heart. So many ways. Your backbone is iron coated, not an iron bar. Otherwise you wouldn't be able to bend. May I continue?"

"Yes."

"Normal humans have blood in their systems, and whenever they need to do something that involves fighting, the hormone adrenaline kicks in. However, you guys are walking tanks of that stuff. As am I, and every other Chosen One who is still alive from their respective generations. Adrenaline courses through your system every hour of everyday from your birth till your death. It makes you impulsive and keeps you awake and active so that you can't be surprised. Even when you sleep, you are aware of your surroundings, ready to move at the first instance. Your brains can process information up to fifteen times faster than a human, assuming you are in peak physical condition. Because of this, you have faster reflexes and can react faster. In battle, you can slow your heart rate all the way down to ten beats a minute so that you can analyse your surroundings better. But your brain will perceive everything in slow motion, so be warned that you can be killed if you use this ability too often. Your brains can retain information and store it, ready at a minutes' notice. Your physical limits are much higher than any human. You can lift ten times your weight, run thrice as fast as a top sprinter, and pull five times your weight. You think you're strong now? You have no idea how much you can do in peak physical condition. And you've not even scratched the surface of your powers."

"That's a lot to take in, Lumenta. How long till we reach PPC?" Ake asked.

Lumenta laughed and said, "Well, PPC is not that far away. As you age, you become stronger and your powers increase. If you lived for about seventy years without realising your powers, your strength would be the same as it is now. With proper training, PPC can be achieved by the time your teens end."

"Ok."

"And now, we are almost done. One last thing about you. Your endurance. The one thing I didn't tell you about your endurance is that you can survive in extremes of climate where humans won't dare to venture. Frostbite doesn't have an effect on you and neither does any illness. That concludes our session. Thank you for co-operating with me. We will begin weapon training after lunch. But before that, remember the protection that one of the Trainers was talking about last night? Well, they're outside just now. Follow me."

Dan had a sneaking suspicion that he knew what protection Lumenta was referring to. Nevertheless, he kept his mouth shut and followed Lumenta outside onto the road. As they turned, Dan nearly had a heart attack. Now he understood why he had sensed eighteen non-human emotions in the morning.

Staring at his friends and him, were three animals from each District of animals; Horses, Ravens, Wolves, Dragons, Lions and Bulls. How they had not made a sound, Dan didn't know. There were about six other Talons standing around the animal group, probably to ensure that they didn't stampede. Ake whistled sharply, and a dark-grey Wolf came out of the group and tackled Ake to the ground.

"Ha-ha. I missed you too, Hadver." Looking at Lumenta, Ake asked, "How did you find him?"

"When we found you, we knew that a Guardian from your Tribe was also there. So it wasn't that difficult to get the Guardian."

Dan looked into the crowd and called, "Frea." A blue roan stallion came out of the crowd and walked up to Dan, nuzzling his nose against Dan's cheek. Dan smiled and looked at Lumenta. "Thank you."

Lumenta just said, "Don't thank me. Thank the Guardian for keeping you safe all these years."

All this while, Emmanuel was standing quietly to the side. He asked Lumenta, "Is it ok if I call my Guardian out? He's a bit cranky."

"Sure, he won't be destructive, I assure you."

Emmanuel stared right into the group and clicked his fingers sharply. A Bull with a broad hump walked out and stopped in front of Emmanuel. He embraced the Bull and said softly, "How are you, Aral?"

The Bull made a soft voice in its throat, as if it understood what Emmanuel had said. Dan was about to ask why the others had not come out, when he heard a rushing noise behind them, coming from the corridor of the building.

Another two groups of boys and one group of girls came out of their buildings. And all hell broke loose.

The Talons moved aside and the animals moved out to greet their respective Chosen Ones. Within one minute, the rest of them came out and it was a mob. Finally, the Trainers herded the Ones back into the buildings, one group at a time. Once in the room, Lumenta started again, "Surely you didn't think that for three hours, I was going to lecture you on yourselves?"

The boys laughed and told him to continue.

"Well, your Guardians are, obviously, from your respective Tribe. They are the embodiment of, as Ake calls it, PPC. They are alike in every way. The Tribes always kept them close by, so that, should anything happen to them, they would look after you. Each Tribe had two breeds of the District's animal. The Ravens have the Black and the Mountain Ravens; the Horses have the Blue Roan and Strawberry Roan Horses; Lions have the friendly Cut Lions and the wild Claw Lions; the Wolves have the friendly Grey Wolves and the almost untameable, Ag-Wolves. The Dragons have the Fire Dragons and Sharp-Winged Dragons, the latter of which can't breathe fire. Finally, the Bulls have the Hump Bulls which are good for labour, and have incredible endurance levels and the Poison Bulls, whose only defence is the poison in their horns."

"So basically, we just got a huge dose of history, didn't we?" Emmanuel said.

"Well, not really. You see, the more you understand your Guardian, the easier it is for you two to fight off threats together, without getting in each other's way. Now, the Guardians from the same District eat the same amount of food. Your animals are Blue Roan Horse, Grey Wolf and Hump Bull. The one difference between Guardians of the same District are their breeds, that's all."

"So, does that mean we can go now, Lumenta?" asked Dan, half hoping that he was right.

"No. I have not finished. Your Guardians will be taken good care of by us. You will be with them during small breaks between programs. They will have their own training here, to ensure that they don't become overweight. We will have friendly competitions from time to time with the other groups till we are sure you can fight off threats properly. Don't bank on your bones to protect you. Strike first, and strike hard. I have faith in you guys. Kill Yedgal, when the time comes, and without hesitation. That's all. Now we have about an hour before lunch, so you can go back to your room. Take your Guardians with you. They will fit. The rooms are enchanted to withstand weights of up to twenty tons and can withstand impacts from rocks thrown at point blank range."

The boys filed out of the room and realised that Lumenta was right; the corridor had become broader; their door was as well. They jumped onto their beds and started introducing their Guardians. Dan didn't normally have a problem with animals, but Ake's Wolf, Hadver, scared him for some reason. He thought about what Lumenta had said about Hadver being a friendly Wolf, but if Hadver was friendly, Dan didn't want to know what the Ag-Wolves were like. Since they had an hour to kill, they took out books titled "How to understand your Guardian". There were pages of their history, their evolution and so on. At last, Dan found a chapter relating to Horses. He went through it, and understood what Lumenta said about them being able to retain information. The chapter was almost a hundred pages, and he finished it in about ten minutes. He saw that his mates had already finished their reading. For a joke, he picked up a book and asked Emmanuel, "Page 167, paragraph 3." Without hesitation, Emmanuel said it. There was another thin book, "How to merge with the Guardian".

Ake took it out and whatever he saw, he didn't like. He looked at Dan and Emmanuel and said, "You read this and tell me if it makes sense."

Emmanuel took the book and read it. After a minute, he said, "This is crazy." He kept the book open and Dan saw pictures of men who were not exactly men. Centaurs, Minotaurs, men with wings and talons, people with muscles too big for them, pictures of them filled the pages. Dan asked, "What is this about?"

Emmanuel read out, "When you and your Guardian are able to understand each other perfectly, they can merge in different ways, according to their District. When a Chosen One and his or her Guardian are in this equilibrium, the spirit of the Horse transfers to the body of the person he or she is guarding.

Depending on how far this equilibrium goes, the Guardian can transfer its spirit for as little as a minute, or as long as a day. This makes the person, to whom the spirit is passed, stronger than he or she is, only in the area where the Guardian and he or she is advanced, apart from the multiplied strength in everyone. After the transfer is over, the Guardian becomes tired, but you are left with a lot of energy. Equines merge with Horses to become Centaurs.

"The same applies to the Taurians, who become Minotaurs. Their strength increases and their skin becomes almost impenetrable due to the elasticity of the skin on the body. Covians join with the spirits of their Ravens, and retain their body structure. But they grow wings and their hands become talons, though there are three fingers on each hand. Leonids combine with the spirits of their Lions and become muscle-bound Manticore berserkers, who like to take out any competition that is in their way. Logdans join to become actual Werewolves, though their thirst for sucking blood is nowhere to be found. They can operate under the darkest night. They are the only ones from the six Districts who can walk out in the open in a combined state and not be suspected by anyone. Lastly, Talons can combine with their Dragons to become indestructible, scale-bound fighting machines. The Dragons' spirit, however, can't help a Talon breathe fire. None of the spirits can help you change into the animal completely. Only its instincts, reflexes and strength is multiplied by yours to give you an edge in a fight."

"That's some serious power to possess, alright. Imagine if you could combine all six Districts' animals in one," Emmanuel said with a whistle.

"There's something based on that also, here." Ake replied. He read out, "If someone were to harness the power of all six

Districts' rings, if he or she were a proper medium without any bias to any District, that person could become one with Lasgalan himself." Ake's face lost a bit of colour. He continued, "Lasgalan is portrayed as the perfect being. He is the embodiment of an ideal harmony of the Districts. He is depicted as an animal with each of the six District's animal's body parts."

Ake stopped reading, aware that both sets of eyes in the room were staring at him with undivided attention. He glanced over to their three Guardians, who were rough-housing in the room, without bringing it down. Desperate to get off topic, as he saw the other two were, he said, "Let's go for lunch. It's almost time."

They went down to the dining room, where most of the other groups were seated. As soon as the last group came in with their Guardians, their plates magically filled up with different amounts of food, as if the plates knew exactly how much their diners were going to eat. There was a silence prevailing over the table and once the last morsel of food was finished, the twenty-four of them were taken to a small building, where there were ten people waiting for them. The girls were whisked off to another room, while the boys were asked to take off their shirts and inner vests so that their chest and stomach were exposed. Dan was waiting for Clint to take off his shirt, as there only four people who knew of his condition. Soon, everyone's shirts were off and just as Dan had expected, everyone was staring at Clint's back. All the boys sported prominent abs, ranging from fourteen-year-old Ake and James to seventeen-year-old Vincent and Emmanuel. More people came in, each taking charge of one boy, who was asked to sit upright on a bed. The doctor in charge of Dan came to him with a clipboard and said, "I am going to ask you some questions and will then conduct some tests on you. Ok?"

Dan nodded.

"Fine. Name, age and District please."

"Dan, fifteen, Equis."

"Thank you, Dan. Now just try to relax." A needle entered his elbow vein. There was no pain though. Some blood came into the vial the doctor was holding. When he was sure he had enough blood, the doctor removed the needle. He handed the blood to his assistant saying, "Report back to me when I'm done."

Shifting his attention back to Dan, he said, "I am going to have to ask you to tell me something about yourself. If you want to, you can answer." He put a pad on either side of Dan's ribcage, and asked him to exhale as much as he could. Dan obliged and soon he was almost over with his tests. As he put his shirt back on, like the others, the doctors' assistants came back, each with a paper that looked like a report. The doctor read through it, looked up at Dan and said, "You are perfectly normal. There is no chance of infection or disease for you. As it is, your metabolism is higher than a human's, so you won't grow fat and put pressure on your heart. You can go now."

Dan was the first to leave the building. As he went out of the door, his eyes fell on a paper that was on the ground. He picked it up and read it.

"Meet me in the library. Third building on the right."

Dan looked around to see if anyone noticed him. He put the paper in his pocket and went back to his room. He took a small arrowhead, just in case it was a trap. Keeping it in his fist, he went back to what he assumed was their hospital, and then went to the library. It was not a small, one story building, but a five-story house that was not divided into floors. The first to fifth floors were just balconies ringing the walls. There were about ten tables on the ground floor, each capable of holding five people with space to spare. As Dan looked around for whoever wrote that letter, another one floated down. This one read: "Third floor." Dan was sure this was a trap, so he exposed a bit of the arrow head, in case he was jumped.

He climbed the first two floors and saw that the balconies too had tables, though they were meant for two people each. As he turned the last corner to the third floor, he suddenly felt compelled to drop the arrow head. He now suspected who had written the letter, and he didn't like it. He climbed the last step and was embraced.

Chapter 23

Victoria felt nervous. She had done nothing of this sort before. But she steeled her nerves and dropped the second letter down to Dan. By the time he came up, she tried to use her vibes to get him to drop whatever was in his fist. When that didn't work, she decided that she was going to have to use more powerful forces. As Dan came up the last step, she waited till he was away from the edge, and embraced him. In that same fluid motion, she kissed him. His lips felt smoother than they looked, and his breath was like cinnamon. For a moment, they knew exactly what to do. Then Victoria came up for a breath and looked at Dan, unsure of what he would say. Before she could explain the sudden embrace, he said, "Victoria, would you be my girlfriend?" He sounded completely honest, as if he was in love.

"Are you…" Victoria started.

"In love with you? Yes."

Victoria laughed silently. She may have been a year older than the fifteen-year-old Equine, but he looked more mature. The way his sideburns came to his jawline, almost hugging the edge; the way he spoke, in a casual yet calculated manner; the way his dark eyes sparkled when he smiled; his blonde hair swept to one side, probably due to Victoria running her hand through it. His hand and leg hairs were almost invisible, so he looked like a waxed man.

Victoria was about to say something else, when someone laughed. He sounded friendly and Dan apparently recognised the voice. He sighed and both of them went to the balcony, and looked down at the ground, where one of Dan's roommates stood. He looked up at them with a smile.

"Well well. What do I see? You lovebirds really need to get a room."

Dan laughed at him and replied, "Shut up, Ake. Don't tell anyone about this."

"Well, that's the second secret I have been asked to keep about love, and I don't keep secrets hidden for long, I'll warn you."

The couple came down the stairs and Ake smiled and asked, "How long have you two been together?"

Victoria smiled and said, "About five minutes."

"Dan, I want a full explanation about why I was not informed about you being in love," Ake joked.

As the three of them turned to the door, Dan's hand in Victoria's, something caught Victoria's eye. It was a piece of wood that had some writing on it, but the script was hard to decipher. Ake said, "I wonder what it says."

A new voice came to them, "It says that this wood will appear when two lovers, destined to be together for life, pronounce their love for each other."

The three turned to see the new comer. He was about fifteen, dressed in a sleeveless shirt, as if he had to wrestle someone. His arm--guards identified him as a Logdan. Ake sighed and said, "Why am I not surprised that you know that, Garon?"

Garon shrugged his shoulders and said, "I am a quick learner. Leave it at that. Anyway, your Trainers want you guys; weapon training is about to commence."

The four of them went to the playing field, where their Trainers were waiting for them. Victoria went to her group, which included Trest and Elesa. They had played volleyball with the boys the previous day, and given them quite the run for their money. As they headed to another field, Victoria kept stealing glances to Dan, who was unmindful of it. She didn't realise where they had reached, until Elesa stopped. They had reached a field that was made like a track-and-field stadium, minus the stands. Tracks were marked out, four hundred metres a round. Hurdles were kept stacked in the centre and weapons of every wood and size were kept to one end of the stadium. In the centre, like a regular athletic stadium, was the range for throwing the hammer, discus and javelin, the same of which were kept in a small enclosure. Victoria remembered her father once talking about Games that were held during Yedgal's reign, where the first three winners of an event were rewarded, but the rest of the competitors were killed on the spot. Those games were held every year, but sometimes even twice a year.

Vulca, her Trainer, spoke with the others for a minute before she came back to them. She told them, "All of us will be making you do an event. You will be given a certain target to get to today. Don't hurt yourselves out there."

"Garon said that weapon training would be today. What about that?" Victoria asked.

"This is weapon training. First get your muscles ready to hold the weapons, then you will hold them."

With that settled, Vulca took them over to the hundred metre mark and said, "The Talons are the fastest runners in Lasgalan. It is either our record you have to beat, or an animal's, depending on the event. The record you have to get to is his." She gestured towards Edward's Trainer and said, "Latyu is fast enough to give a Wolf chase for some time before he wears out. He is not a Chosen One, but he looks the part."

The girls lined up and stared down the track. They braced and ran. They barely reached top speed and finished the race in about fifteen seconds. They headed back and saw Vulca looking at them in disapproval.

"Very poor. You shouldn't have started in a standing position. You lose a lot of energy by standing. Start like them."

Edward's group lined up. Before starting, they dug a bit of earth out in a hole and put their feet in them. When they were released, they shot down the track faster than the girls, but made it in only fourteen and a half seconds. The timekeepers were their Trainers. The fastest down the hundred was Ake's group, clocking in at thirteen seconds.

Once all groups had finished the hundred metres, they were moved to the two hundred metres. After that was the four hundred, where everyone made the mistake of running at top speed, or whatever speed they had left after running the other two races at top speed.

As the last group finished, the Guardians were brought out and were placed at different marks, except the Dragons and the Ravens, whose elements were the air. The Wolves were placed at the four hundred metre mark, while the Horses were placed at the hundred and fifty metre mark. As they were released, the Wolves ran as fast they could, casually overtaking the Lions at the two hundred metre mark and the Bulls at the same. The

Horses had a significant head start on the Wolves, but the latter overtook the Horses ten metres from the finish.

Edward's Trainer, Latyu, came out to address the gathering.

"What I saw today was absolute arrogance. You people can't even run fast enough. I'm not a Chosen One, yet I can easily outrun you, with you guys having a head start. The adrenaline in your bodies is not being put to proper use."

As the crowd dispersed, the Trainers held a short conference among themselves and then followed the youths back to the playing field. They were taken to their rooms, Trainers behind. As they sat down on the beds, Lumenta said, "You already know about merging, right?"

"Yes, how do you know?"

"I just do. Now, can you merge with your Guardians?"

Ake said, "I can try, but I can't guarantee anything."

Lying down on the bed and closing his eyes in concentration, Ake looked like a fitful sleeper. Hadver came and curled up next to his bed. For a few seconds, nothing happened. Then a small green smoke-like wisp emerged from Hadver and slowly travelled to Ake. It hit his chest and he opened his eyes in shock to see the last of it disappear under his shirt. His black eyes flared green and he sat up.

"How you feeling, Ake?" Emmanuel asked.

"Like I can run all day."

Lumenta stared warily at the boy and said, "You're not feeling any different, are you?"

"Except for the fact that I have a Wolfish spirit in me? No."

Ake stood up and extended his hand. His nails, which he kept short, slowly elongated till they were about two inches long. Looking into the mirror on the door, Ake realised that from the outside he had not changed much. Same blonde hair, same physique, only his eyes had gone from black to green. His teeth had become suspiciously canine, but he didn't want blood.

Facing the six, he glanced at Hadver, who was contentedly snoring away. The other two animals backed up a foot from where they were. Ake said, "Do I get a link with Hadver?"

Emmanuel said, "According to the book, a telepathic one."

"Hmm. Let me see." Ake tried to get his Guardian to wake. Instantly, Hadver's eyes opened and he was on his feet. Ake suddenly felt his knees wobble, and would have fallen on his face had Lumenta not grabbed him.

"What was that?"

"Equilibrium was short." Dan said. "Your bond is strong, but not that strong. I'm going to try now."

And he succeeded. Frea and he were pulled together in flash of blue, and when the light shut off, they were looking at a Centaur with the upper body of Dan grafted neatly to his Guardian's torso. His eyes were electric blue and his shirt had been ripped to show his abs and barrel chest. He smiled at his companions and said, "This feels great. The power in my body, it feels awesome." Dan reared up and brought his hooves down on the floor, hard. A sound like a thunderclap was heard, and Dan shouted, "My hooves, my hooves!"

Then he too lost control and reverted back to his regular self. Laughing hysterically, he pointed at Emmanuel and said, "You do it."

Emmanuel's merging went faster than the other two's. His arms looked a bit too big for his shirt and his legs looked like small pillars. He looked scary and Lumenta said, "What do you feel?"

"Anger. Lots of it."

"No doubt. Your horns can regenerate, but you can't hide them. You just became eighty kilograms of pure muscle. Your hands can punch through almost anything, but on the down side, you are not a berserker. You will feel pain, however little. You will get tired, but your skin is almost impenetrable."

Emmanuel snarled at the other two Guardians, but they snarled right back at him. He laughed and willed himself back to his original self. "How did we manage to merge for so long, with no practise?"

"You have been with your Guardian for so many years, you share a certain bond."

As the sun went towards its evening shift, Lumenta asked them to stay in their room.

"Something's not right. It's too quiet."

The boys didn't find anything amiss, but they stayed in their room till an hour after sunset. They had their dinner and were about to talk about something, when there was a golden flash of light that came from the opposite bank of the river. The boys looked out from the balcony, only to see darkness. They were not the only ones curious about the light; they could see, through the torch-lights on the side of the building, their friends trying to figure out what was facing them. Garon shouted, "About forty guys, heavy weapons."

They could see Talons running towards the bridge, but not setting foot on it. The new group must have thrown something at the bridge, because an invisible force-field erupted in a flash of yellow. The Talons tensed, not making sudden moves. The

Guardians growled in their respective rooms, indicating that they did not like the entry of the new company at the doorstep.

Emmanuel got a wild idea and turned to his roommates.

"Shall we merge? We have the same instinct, to survive."

Dan said, "It's worth a shot."

Two minutes later, a Wolf, a Werewolf, a Centaur and a Minotaur dropped down to the ground, next to the Talons. The latter looked at them and whistled in appreciation.

"Let's finish this. We don't know how long we can keep this up."

Just then, the force-field cracked like glass, and the newcomers charged across the bridge. Hadver charged to meet them, followed by the three "merged Ones" and the Talons. Within two minutes, the fight was over and they walked back to their end of the bridge. Emmanuel heard Reidan say, "That seemed easy."

Someone replied, "Actually."

Then the buildings behind the residential ones exploded.

CHAPTER 24

As the triumphant heroes walked back, James couldn't shake the feeling that something was about to go down, something that was going to change him and the rest of his company forever. Then it happened.

The buildings behind theirs' and the girls' exploded in green smoke. He had seen this once before, and wasn't happy to see it again. Chris' mother had died because she had tried to shield Chis and himself from it. James began to realise, that, behind each of his friends' smiling faces, there must be a sad secret of losing a loved one.

Below, the three "merged Ones" changed into three Chosen Ones, plus their Guardians. Half the Talons ran to the fire, while the other half ordered the Chosen Ones down to the ground. Once they had assembled, they were taken to the playing field and told to run as far as they could, as fast as they could, away from the town. They were about to protest when a Trainer, Sens, said, "Ake, Dan, Emmanuel, keep them safe and teach them whatever you know."

With that the rest of the Talons ran back, leaving the Ones no choice but to flee. Ake shouted, "Get to the woods." There was a wood about five hundred metres ahead of them and they ran for it, Guardians forming a small protective circle around them.

With all of them safely in the woods, Dan said, "We should stick together for some time, at least till sunrise. The Guardians will protect us while we sleep." But none of them were ready to sleep, all of them being charged with adrenaline. Garon went to the edge of the woods and peered down the gentle slope that they were on, to the little Talon town they had called "Home". He came back saying, "Whoever those guys are, they've massacred the residents and are staying put for now. But I think they will move out in search of us at first light."

"Cowards," came a voice from the group. Dan stood to the side glaring at the smoke now coming from the town.

"We should have stayed and fought with them, not run away."

"There's nothing we can do now, Dan. Let's first focus on getting away from here. How far is it to the Capital?"

"We will never get there in time," said Edward. "The Capital is maybe a two, two-and-a-half-day journey, by carriage; less than two days by chariot. We don't even have our weapons to defend us."

"Actually, we do," said Karen. All eyes turned to her. "Look."

There were six people who, none had noticed earlier, had rings on their fingers, which they claimed were given to them by their Trainers.

"The Rings of the Districts," they said. There was Logder's Emerald, Leonis' Fire Opal, Equis' Rhodonite, Tauris' Amethyst, Covis' Schorl and Talis' Citrine.

"What will they do?" Ake asked.

"Forgot, Ake?" Garon asked. "Faldor said that these Rings were very powerful, unscorchable, and so on and so forth."

"My dad too said something like that," Emmanuel said.

"But our first problem will be food," James intervened. "If we are two days from the Capital, we will starve before we get there, and possibly die, since our metabolism is higher than a human's."

Then Jacob came up with a brilliant solution.

"Let two Wolves and two Lions go ahead of us and bring down whatever meat they can get their paws on. That should sustain us for two days, if they do it at regular intervals."

"It's worth a shot," replied Trest. "The Ravens and the Dragons can fly overhead, letting us know if the path ahead is clear."

"And weapons?" Edward asked again.

"I think our hands will be enough."

So, the twenty-four of them walked along in a small circular formation, deeper into the woods. They decided to cover as much ground as they could before they rested for the night. When they finally stopped, they had covered about two leagues and were very tired. Their Guardians spread themselves around in a circle that covered every possible entry point. The Dragons, despite their slightly larger size, fitted in nicely, blending in with the dark shadows. If anyone glanced towards them, they would see nothing. But the people on the other side of the Dragon would know if somebody was there. The Wolves walked around with the Lions, their eyes glowing like miniature coloured torches. The Bulls did the same as the Dragons, while the Ravens perched on the trees above. The Horses stood ramrod straight and slept. As they settled down, Ake suggested that the girls sleep in the centre and the boys on the outside of their small circle. Elesa gave Ake a quizzical look, but went to the centre and within two minutes the girls were fast asleep. The boys held a quick conference after that.

Gonth started off, "We should choose our leader. He or she can guide us till the end of our journey."

Edward spoke up, "I nominate the Mergers. They are strong and can fend off a fighting force without weapons."

Robert turned to Dan and asked, "Can you guys teach us how to merge? That way, we can all be ready to fight without weapons."

Ake turned and said, "We will teach you guys everything, don't worry. But right now, let's focus on staying alive."

Vincent was leaning against a tree, staying silent all this time. He glanced at Ake and asked, "Wouldn't it be better if we split up into three groups of eight each? Those guys would have to split up as well. The Guardians would be able to defend us, and if each of you Mergers are there in a group, it would be better for us."

"No. The problem with merging is that, apart from the Wolves, the Guardian actually merges with you. So you lose that many fighters."

"Ok. Let's sleep it out. We better cover at least ten leagues tomorrow."

And with that, the boys too crashed out, though Ake, Dan and Emmanuel kept awake, wondering how they were going to keep their group alive.

CHAPTER 25

In the morning, the first to wake up were the Mergers. They glanced at the rest of their group, who were sleeping soundly. Their Guardians had evidently taken a shift during the night, since the Wolves and Lions were sleeping while the Bulls and Horses were awake and moving around the group.

Ake motioned for the other two to move away from the group, since he would disturb them with the conversation that he wished to have with the duo. The sky was slowly lighting up, but the sun was not even on the horizon. As they trio moved away from the group, Frea accompanied them, as if to make them feel safe.

Dan started, "How are we going to feed them? Our carnivores are sleeping and when the others wake up, they are going to be very hungry."

"It's not light yet," came a new voice from above. "You can send the Wolves for hunting."

The three glanced up to see a Leonid sitting on a branch above them. On his right hand's ring finger, he wore a Fire Opal Ring that looked as if it had flames in it. He dropped down silently and said, "Name's Patrick, in case you forgot. What I was saying was, let the carnivores go. They can track down prey easier than in the dark. As it is, ninety percent of Lasgalan's animals sleep at night."

Ake went carefully to Hadver and tried to wake him with the telepathic link that he thought wouldn't work. But it did. Soon, all three Wolves and two Lions were off into the decreasing darkness, the lives of twenty-four people dependent on them. Emmanuel gazed towards the east and said, "How far do you think we can go before we are overtaken?"

Patrick shrugged his shoulders and said, "Don't know about that. Hopefully my distraction pays off and sends them in another direction."

That got everyone's attention.

"What distraction?"

Pointing to the north, Patrick said, "Look at the trees."

Sure enough, there was smoke rising above the trees, as if a fire had started.

"I used my Ring to start a fire. It may be my element, but I did not expect it to work so well."

"Let's just hope that they actually buy it." Emmanuel said.

Just then there was a rustling sound behind them, but it turned out to be just a Raven. Patrick asked, "Guys, what are your weapons of choice?"

"Axe, bow and club. Why?"

Patrick closed his eyes and stretched out his hands. From his Ring, fire shot out until there was a straight fire across his palms. When the flames died out, Patrick was holding an axe, identical to Ake's. He tossed it and Ake, catching it, asked, "How?"

"I went down to the armoury on the first day and saw their weapons. Now, I only have to visualise something and it becomes a reality thanks to the Ring." He did the same for the other two and was talking till they saw the sun coming up. Just then, Emmanuel asked, "Patrick, you are a regular human, right?"

"Yes. I don't have any gifts like you guys, but I am a good strategist."

"I suppose we should wake the others, now that food's come." Dan interrupted. Sure enough, heading for them were the five carnivores, their mouths full with deer and goat.

The four of them went around awakening everyone and soon, all were up. Patrick gathered some sticks and lit them up, while Clint cut and roasted the animals on a spit. Being in the army, he said, he was prepared for every situation that could arise if he was left out in the open. As they ate, the early risers filled the rest of them in on their conversation. People looked at Patrick's Ring and asked him how to produce weapons. Soon, everyone had their respective weapons by their side, courtesy of the other Ring wielders.

They were about to start off again when Ake put his hand up and said, "Stop! Everybody freeze."

They did so, wondering what was going on. But Ake could hear it. There was a thundering sound, soft at first, but getting louder by the second. Afraid that their pursuers had seen their fire, Patrick quickly threw dirt on it to mask the smoke. As Ake glanced around, he saw them galloping hard towards Patrick's distraction.

Once they were out of sight, Ake said, "No more walking till I say so. We run from now."

And with that, they were off. The Lions and Wolves brought up the rear of their group, the Bulls ahead of them and the Horses and Ravens flanked the group. The Dragons had disappeared into the sky and weren't seen after that. The group made a lot of sound, scaring off numerous birds in the process and probably giving away their location. But they didn't care. All they wanted was to get some distance away from the riders. After an hour or so, everyone started to tire. The regular humans were already riding the Horses and Bulls. The Guardians too slowed down. Finally, Dan made everyone stop. There was a river up ahead that dropped down a hundred metres before flowing into a vast clearing. Across the clearing, they could see about fifty or so Dragons, all moving around peacefully, as if they had all the time in the world. But the real problem was ahead of them.

"How are we going to get from up here to down there?" Vincent asked, gesturing to the hundred metre drop with his javelin. Ake realised that he had led his group into a trap. If the riders came now, they would be wedged between the waterfall and the riders. Then came the solution.

"Step aside, little brother," Hasha told Ake. "I got this."

This got Ake a few snickers. But he watched as his sister closed her eyes and clenched her fists tightly. Then she said, "One by one, everybody jumps into the river." No one argued. Chris went first. As he jumped in, a small wave arose from the river and carried him down the fall and onto dry land. Then went Elesa, then Vincent, then the rest of the girls. As the last girl came onto land, Hasha said, "I can't do anymore; I feel tired."

"Well then, I guess you wouldn't mind dying saving your friends," came a familiar voice behind them.

Ake whirled around, swinging his axe at the man's face, but he darted out of reach.

Hoping to buy his sister some time to take the others down, Ake spoke up, "Where is your little gang?"

"Oh, I come alone, with a separate mission. I just have to take a few of you along with one District Ring. It's your choice which one you want to give. If you refuse, well, I have means of getting what I want. I am not an unreasonable person." Saying so, he pulled out a bow from behind him and nocked an arrow, pointed it at Ake and said, "The Ring please."

Ake laughed at him and said, "Fat chance."

The man shrugged and said, "Fair enough."

He turned his bow and shot it at Hasha. The force was too much and she was thrown backwards, to the edge of the cliff. Garon lunged out to catch her, but she slipped from his hand and fell down the cliff.

Before anyone could react, Edmund pushed Garon down the cliff and went down with him. Ake yelled and brought his axe down with full force on the ground. From the axe, a crack snaked out and headed for the man, who turned and ran into the jungle.

Meanwhile, Garon plunged after Hasha. As he neared her, he felt a strange power enter his body. He shot out his hand and grabbed Hasha's. As the base came closer, the wind pushing them up, Garon pulled her upwards, so that he came below her, like a cushion for the landing. He hit the water, hard. As he got buoyed up, he realised a few things. He was not dead, he hadn't broken any bones, Hasha was fine and Edmund was missing. He swam Hasha to the shore, where two girls helped her up, and dived under the water. He went till a depth of about twenty metres and tried to see through the darkness of the water. When he didn't see anything, he went up again and swam to the shore. Once he climbed up, he noticed that people were giving him strange looks. He glanced back to the top of the falls, wondering what happened to the others.

Then, he saw a Centaur run off the cliff and land just ahead of him, two people on his back.

As his passengers got off, Dan turned to Garon and said, "Welcome to the party." At first Garon couldn't understand what he was talking about. Then it dawned on him.

"But how? This didn't happen to Ake when he did it."

"No idea. But anyway, at least you didn't die trying to pull off that stunt. Speaking of which...," He bent down and whispered to Garon. "Is she your lady love?"

"No. She does have a crush on me though."

"I see. Well, here come the next lot."

As he said that, Emmanuel dropped to the ground, five people in tow. They all got off and two of them, namely Clint and James, went to the river and retched. Ake came down with one person. Garon asked, "How are the others coming down?"

Ake replied, "Watch."

He stepped into Garon's shadow and disappeared. After a minute the remainder of the group came down with him, along with Hadver. The Guardians, Ake said, would find their own way down to them, and that they should start moving. The Dragons didn't stop them, but didn't even pay attention to them as they walked through. Towards midday, the other Guardians made it to them and then they only walked. At one point, Dan got fed up and turned to Edward.

"How much further?"

Edward smiled for the first time and said, "Actually, we are on a shortcut. We should reach there by tonight or by tomorrow morning. Once we are there, I don't think anyone will stop us."

"Couldn't tell us that sooner, could you?" Dan muttered. Being in Centaur form, he was taller than the rest and had to bend low to talk to them, and it was really hurting his back. Soon they stopped for water and were feeling very hungry. This time the carnivores didn't have to go very far. There was tasty duck ahead of them, which they caught with their own hands.

Once they had finished, they continued on their way. The Mergers unmerged and kept walking. They stopped twice before evening and had covered about five leagues until sunset. They had to cross a small stream when Ake heard leaves crackling as if someone was stepping on them. He wouldn't have paid attention to it, if it was not a faint and slow sound. That meant they were being followed. He said nothing but slowly drifted to the back of the group. He looked around and noticed hair sticking out from behind a bush. He crept behind their stalker, unknown to the latter. He placed his axe on his neck and whispered, "One move and you're dead." To Ake's astonishment, the one under the axe calmly stood up, turned to face him and pushed away the axe blade.

"You are most welcome to kill me, Ake. But who will guide you on your journey after that?"

"Why didn't you come to us earlier?"

"First I had to track you, then I had to make sure I wasn't being tracked."

"We have been walking the past two days, hoping to get to the Capital. You want to come with us?"

"Sure. Thanks."

CHAPTER 26

G aron was quite shocked when he turned around to ask Ake a question, only to find him not there in the group. As his sharp eyes scanned their surroundings, he noticed Ake coming towards them with someone they had met earlier on, at Shodor. He watched as the two of them came forward, and the others also turned in that direction.

They came up to the group and Ake said, "No need to panic. Jax here is a friend."

"Hello everyone," Jax said in a relaxed manner, as if he encountered two dozen heavily armed individuals every day. "I am coming with you to the Capital, and after that, I will most probably leave you to fend for yourself. Now that we have got that out of the way, let us move on, shall we?"

"Sounds good enough for me." Garon replied. They set off again and the Guardians seemed relaxed as well. They spread out in a larger circle and didn't glance around for danger. They cleared a small grove and when they came onto the other side, they saw a forty-foot granite wall towering over them. Since it was quite dark, there were torches alit on the ramparts and also on the towers that were atop the walls, as they could see the orange glow of fire. As they approached the gates, they tried to push it open, but it was bolted up from the inside. Emmanuel took care of that. He merged and gave the two doors a slight push and created a gap wide enough to allow two people to pass through together. As he was the last one through, he stepped forward and let the gates close behind him with a loud BOOM! That got the attention of the guards stationed at the top of the wall. They surrounded the small group and held up their spears, keeping them at a safe distance away from themselves. Emmanuel hadn't unmerged, but even his strength was waning. If it came down to a fight, he would be the first one on the ground.

Fortunately, it did not come down to a fight. Jax raised his hands and said, "It is ok guys. We come in peace."

One of the guards was not convinced of that as he shouted, "Prove it. Weapons down, now!"

Ake was about to drop his axe when another guard walked up to them and said, "That will not be necessary. You are being summoned to the palace by Lord Veryu. She will see you and then decide your fate."

The other guards dropped their spears and walked in a protective ring around them. The city was still quite awake and some people eyed the two dozen teenagers and tried to get closer to them. However, the guards levelled their spears at them and sorted the matter out. After about ten minutes of walking, they came up to the palace and were left to go inside. As they headed down the corridors of the palace to the throne room, they were astounded by what they saw. Paintings and priceless chandeliers stole the show. But what some of the girls noticed were the sceneries of different parts of Lasgalan. They showed events that were occurring in the same time as the girls were watching.

They approached the throne room and were silenced. The ceiling was maybe thirty feet high and decked in gold and silver. In the centre stood a map of Lasgalan showing every

District and each feature in them. The sides of the circular room had pairs of pillars with the District Lords' statues in between two of them. Between each pair of pillars, was a door, flanked by two guards. One of these doors was the one they had just walked through. Ahead of them were steps leading up to two thrones, one large and one slightly smaller. On the larger throne sat a woman who looked as if she was in her mid-thirties. Her brown hair stood out against her white skin, making Victoria mutter, "I wish I had hair like hers." Dan heard this and glanced towards his girlfriend. Victoria was fair, though not as much as the lady on the throne. But he liked that. He liked people as they were. He did not like them changing themselves to look better. His logic was: "You were made the way you are for a reason. Embrace it."

The lady wore a simple green dress that looked quite nice on her, though it looked a bit tight. Dan, being the gentleman that he was, said nothing, and hoped everyone was sensible enough to do the same. He was not anxious to be thrown into Talon jail.

They reached the centre of the room and stopped, waiting for someone to say something.

The lady started off, "I am Lord Veryu, District Lord of Talis. I have seen you coming for some time now, and am frankly quite impressed that you have managed to make a Dark General run away without his prize. You will be given rooms for the night and your Guardians will be taken care of properly. Jax, you will be given a separate quarter to sleep in. Now Emmanuel, if you would kindly unmerge. All your questions will be answered tomorrow."

Emmanuel and Aral had separated and Aral looked exhausted, more than any other Guardian. The animals and their owners were taken in two separate directions. The Ring-bearers were taken to one room, the remaining girls to another, the Mergers to one and the rest of the boys were in another room. All rooms were on the same corridor and Dan joked that this made it easy for him to sneak into Victoria's room and then walk the palace with her. Their escorts laughed and dared him to try it, for they would be patrolling that same corridor, ready to stop him from doing so.

The four boys jumped on their beds and proceeded to talk amongst themselves. Ake asked Garon, "How come Edmund didn't remain back when you merged with him?"

"No idea. But the power surge felt good. I think that is what saved me from broken bones at the bottom of the fall. Still, at least I know what it is like now to have an animal in myself."

Dan turned to Emmanuel and said, "If we have to train the others, we should first teach them merging. Then they will be able to defend themselves."

"True," Garon replied. "But you guys at least have an ability that pertains to an animal. Even Emmanuel's got an advantage. You don't back down from a fight, that's also an animalistic trait. My speciality is my eyes, how does that fit in with an animal?"

"Wild animals need better eyesight to see through thick wooded areas, that's where you come into play. You and James are the least likely to be caught on a stealth mission. You will see the enemy coming, and James can turn invisible at will."

"Good point. Anyway, should we sleep now, considering the work ahead of us is going to be hard."

Ake laughed as he pulled up his covers, "Ha! Teaching fourteen people at the same time. Whatever could go wrong?"

"Oh, shut up and sleep," Garon commanded. As he put his head down, the torches snuffed themselves out.

CHAPTER 27

The four Mergers woke up at the crack of dawn, with the sky turning from black to grey. Their door was a bit ajar, allowing a bit of cool air through the room. They saw that there were clothes already kept for them. They bathed, changed and got out of their room and saw the night-time patrollers walking up and down the corridor. The other three rooms had not woken up yet. The guards allowed them to wake the others up. Dan stood at the door of the girls' room and saw the six girls sleeping soundly. He was about to risk his life by what he was about to do, but he didn't care. Taking a deep breath, he shouted at the top of his lungs, "GIRLS!! WAKEY, WAKEY!! IT'S NICE AND SUNNY!! GET UUUUUP!!"

The result was worse than he imagined. One scythe came out of nowhere, narrowly missing him and impaling itself on the pillar behind him. Looking back at the room, he saw all six of them up and glaring at him, Victoria looking like she was ready to kill him.

Smiling broadly at them he said, "Good morning ladies." He bowed low to them and backed up behind the door-frame.

Ake had gone to the room with the rest of the boys, who were also sleeping. He shouted, "EVERYONE UP!! BREAKFAST IS SERVED!!"

Everyone shot out of their beds and looked around for the breakfast, which of course, was not there. Ake laughed and said, "Get ready. Then we will see about breakfast."

James glared daggers at Ake and said, "If you were not my friend, you would have this in your stomach by now." He lifted his knives and pointed them at Ake.

Meanwhile, Garon had gone to the Ring-bearers' room. He clapped once, didn't get a response, and then yelled, "WAKE UP!! IT IS ALREADY AFTERNOON!! GET UUUP!!"

The next thing Garon knew, he was on the floor, courtesy a wall of water from Hasha's Emerald. Laughing, he got back on his feet and told the others in the corridor, "Yes they are up and raring to go."

Dan smiled back and saw Emmanuel walking down the corridor. The sun was almost on the horizon and there were soon twenty-four youngsters ready to eat. They were escorted back to the throne room, now empty and walked across to a door placed between the pillars that housed the statues of the Lords of Equis and Leonis. They were soon walking down a small corridor that overlooked the rest of the Capital. Below, in the city, people were going about their business, though Garon, with his sharp eyes, could see some of them looking up at the Palace. They reached the dining hall, which was just like the one they had eaten in with their Trainers. The irony made his heart hurt, because he enjoyed his Trainer's company, even if it was just for two days. He was about to sit down when Lord Veryu walked in. She gestured for them to sit down and as they were eating, she asked, "I trust that you had a good sleep?"

Everyone nodded.

"Good, because from today your Trainers will be putting you to the test."

That got everyone's attention. But she waved her hand away and said, "I will let them explain it to you."

Finishing their meal, the teenagers went back to their rooms to collect their weapons and went again through the throne room, through another door into a large field that looked like the one they had practised in before. The only difference was that there was no volleyball court. There was only a basketball court and a football field.

At the middle of the field stood, as promised, their old Trainers. They had a lot of battle scars, from their previous battle. As they walked up, the eighteen power-houses saw that their eighteen pets were also there, looking absolutely refreshed. The Dragons must have come sometime in the night, since they had not entered with the group.

As they gathered round, Patrick asked the question on everyone's mind, "Sens, how?"

Patrick's Trainer smiled and pointed at Garon, "You, my friend, should not always believe what your eyes show you. Did you honestly think that we would be defeated like that?"

"Then what about the group of riders who chased us?"

"Oh, they must have been assassins. They are not found unless they want to be found."

"So how did you escape? It looked like they had killed you."

"We used Argentic transporters to teleport ourselves to the Capital. The others said that they would hold them off. Those are the ones who you saw dead. Lord Veryu wanted us to stay here and wait for you to come to us."

"Of course, we wanted to come and get you, but since our loyalty lies to the Lord of Talis, there was nothing we could do," said one of the female Trainers.

The conversation over, the Trainers said, "The first thing you need to learn, apart from you Ring-bearers, is how to merge. Ake, Garon, Dan and Emmanuel will teach you how to do so. Boys, the field is yours."

The four of them faced their friends. Ake started off, "First of all, I would like each of you to stand three metres away from each other. Now, all you Guardians can go to each of your respective Ones. Dan, you're up."

"Right. The first thing you have to know is that, for you and your Guardian to merge, you must be thinking on the same level. That is just for now. Once you and your Guardians are comfortable enough with each other, you could read each other's minds and maintain the merge for a longer time. I don't expect you to hold this for longer than a few minutes, so please prove me wrong. Emmanuel, your turn."

Emmanuel stepped forward and said, "When you merge, both your bodies become one, except for Wolves, where the Guardian stays out as a separate entity. But, for Garon it didn't happen. But for Ake, well, he can show you himself. Ake, please show us."

Ake crouched down next to Hadver and closed his eyes in concentration. This time, Dan didn't see the green wisp escape from Hadver, but Ake's eyes flared green again and smiled at the learners' group. The first row of Guardians backed up and growled at him, because now they could see his very sharp teeth and two-inch nails.

Hadver stretched his neck as if nothing had happened. Suddenly, he sprung at Dan, putting him on the ground. Getting up, Dan asked Ake, "Was that necessary?"

"No. Though I needed to teach Elesa about the telepathic link we share." Looking at her, he said, "Yes, you heard me right. You can talk to your Guardian via your mind. This helps in dire situations, where speaking takes too long."

Elesa crossed her arms and said, "Please continue."

Emmanuel went on, "Each District merging is different so you will get different attributes. At first, you may feel that you are contesting for control over the body, but you have to strike a balance. Think of your mind as a coin balancing on a tightrope; it should not tilt one way or the other. It should roll straight down the rope."

"So how will we manage to keep a balance, if it is an animal's mind against ours?" Isabella raised a question.

"Good question, Isabella. The thing is, you and your Guardian have been together for years, so your bond will be strong. You might be able to hold your form for a few minutes. Even the three of us, on our first attempt on merging, couldn't hold our form for long. Don't worry about failing, I have faith in you."

Ake then intervened, "Right, let's get you merging, first attempt. We will be there to help you, advise you, but you have to go the extra league and put in the effort. The faster you get to a proper merge, the better your chances of survival outside these walls. Let's go!!"

The first merging, which was a half an hour session, didn't go so well, but better than any of the four could have thought. Vincent managed to hold his form the longest, about two minutes. He sprouted a thick layer of hair around his neck, almost like his Lion's mane, which was golden in colour. His arms became thicker, and he roared like a Lion. Gonth, on the other hand didn't do so well. He and his Guardian had barely merged for a few seconds, then he lost his concentration and fell to the ground. Undeterred, he got up and tried again. This time he held his form longer than Vincent, for a good five minutes. Ake whistled appreciatively and glanced at the eight Trainers, who were teaching the Ring-bearers how to use their Rings properly. Meanwhile, Garon had merged, and was taking on the ones who had managed to hold their respective forms for longer than a minute, he fought five fights, winning all but one, when he had to face Elesa. In his defence, he said, it was difficult to fight a girl and not injure her, while she did not have any compulsion of not hurting him, while she had her Guardian fight him at the same time.

The Dragons didn't go through much of a physical change, though their arms became lined with scales, which could hold off almost any weapons' attack. But they claimed that they had scales on their legs and almost everywhere on their bodies, except the face and neck, where they were not worried of any attack hitting them, since any weapon would shatter on impact with their bones.

After a while, Garon could not hold his form. Edmund and he separated after a fight with Edward and Ontemp, a Fire Dragon. His claws had not even scratched Edward's scales. He squatted and tried to steady his breathing, while Edmund curled up into a ball and lay flat on the ground. Dan filled in for Garon, going into Centaur form and knocking the wind out of Isabella and her Guardian, Esquire. Esquire too was a Blue Roan Horse and she was as big as Frea, which was not common. Usually in Lasgalan, the male side of any species were larger than their female counterparts. Unlike Dan, whose clothes had been magically removed to reveal his chest and stomach, Victoria only had her stomach exposed, while she retained the rest of her clothes. Looking around for anyone else who needed help merging, Dan started to notice that all their

Guardians were of the same size and structure, within their respective Districts of course.

Just then, he got called by Robert, whose Guardian was a Strawberry Roan Horse called Darius. Robert said that whenever they merged, Darius kept trying to take full control of his mind. Dan asked him to try again, since he was there to help them strike a balance. This time, they merged all right, though the next instant Dan found himself facing a Centaur with full body armour, unlike Isabella and himself. The only thing missing was a helmet. He faced Dan and said, "We are managing to keep this form stable. Now, let's duel."

"My pleasure, pal."

Before Dan could do anything, Robert grabbed his shoulders and reared up, leaving Dan's rear hooves just above the ground. He then said, "Forgot that I excel at hand-to-hand combat?"

Dan smiled at him and replied, "Forgot that I am a berserker?"

Robert didn't show any fear, neither did Dan sense any coming off him. Dan used his rear hooves to get a hit at Robert's chest and using the same momentum, freed himself from his opponent's grip and executed a perfect flip, landing back on his hooves. However, Robert was not finished. He charged Dan and hooked his left arm across Dan's neck, not allowing the arm-guards to touch him. However, even without the stun of the metal, Dan was on the floor. He almost unmerged, feeling Frea's strength almost pushed to the limit. Nevertheless, he accepted Robert's hand and congratulated him on successfully merging and fighting without a problem.

Robert looked at Isabella and said, "How about you and me, in a one-on-one battle?"

Isabella shrugged and said, "Don't mind."

The duo circled each other in Centaur form. The others backed up so that they wouldn't be on the receiving end of their rear hooves. As they sized each other up, it looked as if it was fire meeting water. Red against blue. Robert was two inches taller than Isabella, but she didn't seem fazed by that. On the contrary, she smiled and said, "It is not too late to back down now."

"Sadly, I don't ever back down from a fight."

They charged each other at frightening speed. They didn't have any weapons in their hands, but that didn't make them any less dangerous. One of them was a skilled combatant when he had to use his hands, and the other one could get him into a trap she lay for him without him escaping from it. They were equally matched and their first clash involved Robert getting thrown ten feet back. He got back up and wiped the streak of blood coming out of his mouth.

"Not bad. You caught me off guard once, which also happens to be the last time. Now, let's get back down to business."

He ran full speed at her and caught her around the stomach. Lifting her up, he said, "Anyone else want to take me on?"

Just then, he felt a drop in his power and barely had time to put Isabella down. He and Darius separated. Sitting up, he patted the back of his now exhausted Guardian and said, "Thanks Darius, you were great."

Garon smirked and said, "Spoke too soon, did you?"

"Oh, shut up."

Jacob, who had merged twice by then, got up and said, "How about a battle, Edward?"

Edward got up and asked, "How badly do you want to get beaten?"

They merged, and Jacob felt a power surge greater than the other two times he had merged with his Guardian, Zoh. Zoh, being a Cut Lion, did not have sharp claws, though his fangs were quite sharp. Jacob realised that Edward was protected by two layers: his Guardian's scales and his own flames. He hoped that he could find a chink in Edward's defences. He stepped up and let his mane grow out. His eyes, like the last two times of merging, flared yellow. He was shorter to Edward by three inches, but his bulk made up for it. In combined form, the two of them did not get an increase in height. As they stared down each other and charged. Zoh's instincts started taking control of Jacob's mind, though he was able to keep them in check. Zoh saw potential competition for the top of the food chain, so did Jacob. He jumped at Edward, ready to bite his throat, but Edward used his main power and burst into flames, singeing Jacob's mane. Jacob roared and swept his legs at Edward, knocking him down to the ground. The next second, he was up and the two combatants circled each other. Then, without warning, Edward burst into flames again, but these were larger and hotter flames than the last time. All the others backed away, except Garon and Emmanuel. Jacob shouted, "Are you mad? You will burn us all!"

"Then so be it."

The heat became unbearable and Jacob knew that he couldn't land a hit at Edward like this. That's when Emmanuel swung into action. Fully merged, he ran to Edward and caught him around the ribs. He said, "Stop this Edward, or I'll crush your ribcage."

Edward's flames shut off, and he went limp in Emmanuel's arms. Emmanuel placed him in the shade of the wall and said, "When he wakes up, tell him to take the rest of the day off."

Just then, two Trainers, Lucia and Reidan came over and said, "Some of you are more gifted than others, even we can see that. There are six of you, one from each District. Robert, Edward, Clint, Garon, Karen and Vincent, please step outside and follow us."

Vincent said, "Edward is knocked out. He can't move."

Reidan looked down at him and said, "Fine. Let him rest. How did he end up like that?"

When he was told, Reidan patted Emmanuel on the shoulder and said, "Well done."

The five of them were taken to a gate which they hadn't seen before. Beyond it was a rolling landscape. Lucia said, "This is a place where you can make full use of your powers without hurting anyone. Now, by all means merge."

"You six are very special too us. None of the twenty-four are expendable, but if it came down to a choice, we would rather have you six surviving to take down Yedgal than the other eighteen. First, we need you to reach the absolute limit of your power."

The five merged, and Karen understood what Reidan was saying. Robert became a fully armoured Centaur, unlike his friends. Garon and his Guardian became one, unlike Ake and Elesa. Clint's Raven joined with him, and he had to remove his footwear as his feet elongated, becoming talons. He grew wings which he later claimed he always had, his thumb and last finger disappeared, while the other three fingers elongated by two inches. Karen joined with her Poison Bull, Qezre, and became two inches taller, more muscular than Emmanuel, and blue flames shot out of her nostrils. Vincent combined with his Guardian, a Cut Lion called Nilesh, and became a full-grown Manticore. His mane grew out thick from his neck, and his eyes became yellow. His arms shortened about an inch and his legs grew by the same amount. His hands became wider and thicker, and when he clapped them together, no sound was heard. He smirked and said, "I just became the ultimate stealth machine."

Clint laughed and said, "No, that title goes to James. He can turn invisible, you sadly cannot."

"You had to step in on my moment, didn't you?" Vincent replied, feigning annoyance.

Robert and Vincent faced off as a trial encounter, as Reidan put it. Karen didn't see how this was going to end well for Vincent. He was a good projectile marksman, not really a fighting machine like Robert. As they charged, Vincent ducked and came up behind Robert, kicking him on the back. Robert didn't appear to feel pain, and turned around to backhand Vincent a good fifteen feet. Vincent got up, a scar on his face running from his ear to his chin. He snarled and said, "Lucky hit." He ran and using his taller frame, jumped over Robert and landed perfectly on his Horse back. Robert reared up and tried to shake his new rider. Vincent knew that he couldn't make a dent in Robert's armour, so he used his superior grip and held onto the armour around Robert's human abdominal region. He said, "I go down, you are going down with me."

Robert reversed the phrase and said, "You are going down on your own, without taking me with you." So saying, he galloped twenty metres at a fast pace and swung his body forwards, using his front hooves as a pivot. Vincent lost his grip and fell flat on his face. He tried to get up, but instead unmerged.

Next, Garon faced off against Karen. Lucia shouted a warning to Garon, "Don't let her horns, nails or teeth touch you. They contain poison potent enough to kill someone like you in a matter of seconds. You won't feel anything though."

Garon nodded and said, "Noted."

He extended his nails and said, "You can't touch me, but I can touch you."

He lunged at her, narrowly missing her face by an inch. His green irises expanded till they covered his entire eye. His black pupils narrowed horizontally and were visible as small slits across the length of his eyes. He snarled like a Wolf and let loose a guttural roar. Facing his opponent, he lunged again at her. This time he managed to get a few strands of her hair.

During all this, Reidan and Lucia were watching. Realising that something was wrong with Garon, Clint was about to step in to save Karen, but Lucia put her arm across, indicating for him to wait. Just then, Garon managed to get Karen on the ground and had managed to hold her nails away from himself. She tried in vain to bring her hands down so that he would, alarmed, release his grip. But he was much stronger than her and didn't release his grip. Deciding that enough was enough, Clint spread his wings and took off from the ground, reached a height of three metres and, swooping down, kicked Garon in the back. His grip released, and Karen ran from him. Clint landed and saw that Garon and Edmund had unmerged, and heaved a sigh of relief. He checked Karen for injuries, though there were no visible ones. He looked at Lucia and Reidan for an explanation, but got nothing. Since he was the only one left, Robert and he faced off against each other.

Robert pounded the earth with his front hooves, showing a demonstration of his power. Clint stretched his wings to full length. He realised that after he had started merging with his

Guardian, a Black Raven called Cyrus, his wings would disappear after he unmerged. His wingspan was six feet, and he stretched his fingers. He knew that he couldn't make a dent in Robert's armour without causing some damage to himself, so he took off from the ground and circled Robert twenty feet in the air. Robert eyed him like a hunter about to take out his prey. Suddenly, Clint swooped down and tried to snag Robert's back in his talons, but the Centaur evaded him gracefully. As Clint went up, Robert laughed and said, "I should warn you that I am a decent dancer, Clint."

"Tell your girlfriend that, please," Clint replied sarcastically. He went down again, but this time in front of Robert, pulling up slightly at the last second, and succeeded in catching the equine part of Robert's back, and picked him up. Robert may have been pulled out of his element, with no room to balance himself, but he started to twist and turn, hoping to imbalance Clint and get him to release his victim. After about ten seconds of struggling, Clint had to give in. He released Robert about ten metres in the air, not much, but a dangerous drop. Robert was about to hit the ground, when a gust of wind blew him sideways, so that he hit the ground gently. He looked over at Reidan, who said, "Next time you guys think about going all out, please tell us so that we can prepare to get you safely back down to earth."

Robert smiled and said, "It would not have hurt me in any case. My skeleton would have taken the impact."

"Don't be so sure. Even the best defences have some defects in them."

Clint flew down and said, "Robert, don't ever do that again."

"Anyway," Karen interrupted. "What are supposed to do with these four?" She gestured to Garon, Vincent and their respective Guardians, all four of whom were on the ground, passed out.

"Hmm. Take them back inside. They may have pushed their limits beyond what their Guardians had to offer them."

Karen asked, "What happened to Vincent was understandable. But Garon?"

Reidan took a total of ten heartbeats to answer.

"He either tried to exercise his power too much, or his Guardian managed to overcome and take control of mind, turning him into a beast."

"You mean that it could happen to us too?" Karen asked.

"Yes. It is more possible for you six to get imbalanced than the other twelve. That is probably what happened to Edward, though he may have just lost control of his Guardian rather than the Guardian taking over his mind. Anyway, let's take these guys back."

Looking over at the four limp bodies, Clint felt his arms hurting. Just to carry one was painful enough, but he decided to pick up the two boys while the others took the Guardians.

Going back to the main space, they saw that Edward was up again, and that the Ring-bearers were using their Rings to great effect and seemed to have mastered the knack of creating objects. He heard Robert whistle and say, "That's fast, considering that they had the Rings for such a short amount of time."

Lucia laughed and replied, "We Talons are quite good at helping people get things done perfectly, fast."

Edward saw them and started to walk towards them. Just then, Vesper seemed to lose control of her Ring and flames shot out at Edward. Before they could say anything, the flames washed over him, leaving everyone watching, shocked. But then, Edward walked out of the flames as if it was an everyday routine for him. He smiled at them and said, "I see that you left me alone and went to practise. I feel wounded." He put the last sentence into a fake voice of hurt.

Reidan said, "Any idea what happened to you?"

"I lost control of my power. It won't happen again, that I can assure you."

Clint saw that Ake and Elesa were talking about something, off in one corner of the courtyard. Being in the army had disciplined him enough not to poke into others' business, but the teenager in him was still alive. He casually walked up to the two of them and put one arm around each of them and said, "Now, what are you two lovebirds talking about?"

The response was two-fold. First, Ake gave him a death-stare. Elesa, on the other hand, smiled shyly and didn't say anything. Ake dragged Clint by the arm out of earshot of Elesa and said, "What did you mean by doing that? Also, how did know that I have a crush on her?"

"Well, I have a friend called Garon who told me. As for your first question, I thought that I could talk you up to her, if you didn't drag me away like this. Anyway, is there any chance I can be her boyfriend instead of you? I am clearly the better choice." He smiled playfully at the end of the last sentence.

"If you want to live to a ripe old age, Clint, back off." Ake spoke in a calm and steady manner.

"It's cool. If you need any relationship advice, you know who I am and where to find me."

Ake glared at Clint for ten heartbeats before Clint walked away, laughing to himself. He walked back to Elesa, but now, for some reason, could not bring himself to look directly into her eyes.

She said, "I know, even I can't look at you. I don't want you to pay attention to what other people say." She put one hand on his shoulder, and Ake felt a shock go through his body. It took all of his willpower not to remove her hand or look at it.

"Yeah, you are right. What matters is what we think of each other. Oh, and I am sorry."

"For what?"

"For doubting your abilities." Ake said. Elesa smirked and punched him in the gut, though not very hard. Ake's liver did not like it at all. He heard someone say, "They make a cute couple. I wonder if we will get invited to their wedding."

Ake understood who had said this, but didn't turn in the direction of the speaker. He would get back at him later. The two of them walked back to the group, now relaxing in the warm sun. Elesa went to talk with Robert about some fighting style, as far as Ake could figure. Just then, Dan came up to Ake and said, "We need to talk, it's urgent."

Ake nodded, indicating Dan to speak.

Dan started off, "I know that you heard that comment. I just want to say that I know what I said was wrong, but I couldn't contain myself. I didn't mean anything wrong; I just want you know."

Ake didn't say anything, but just stared across to where Robert and Elesa were talking. Their conversation involved a lot of hand waving and Ake wondered whether they were communicating in sign language or actually talking to each other.

"Do you think Robert would make a better companion for Elesa?"

"Hey, don't say that. She likes you and you like her. But if you want me to do my speciality on Robert, I will do it for you."

Ake didn't say anything, but just nodded slightly. Dan closed his eyes and said, "Sorry about this Robert."

Since he couldn't single out Robert's emotions without getting others', he sat down. He didn't want to be overwhelmed by so many people, but managed to get Robert. That "feedback" was so devastating that Dan immediately opened his eyes and shut out every emotion he was receiving. Tears built up on the edges of his eyes, but he didn't cry. Ake asked him, "Well?"

"You don't ever have to worry about him trying to take Elesa away from you, that I can assure you."

"Why? What did you see in there?"

"I want to erase that from my memory. I don't want to experience that ever again."

Clint came to the five of them, since they were sitting a little away from the main group and said, "We are going in for lunch. You guys need to come with us."

"Where's freedom when you need it?" Ake feigned annoyance.

Clint chuckled and said, "Be happy you are not in the army. You see your family for one month in the entire year. And if your District is threatened, you better be ready to fight day and night. Don't talk about freedom, especially when you have it."

As they headed in, Dan wondered to himself, "Will Victoria leave me for someone else? Am I actually good enough for her?"

With these thoughts in his mind, he walked into the building for his meal.

CHAPTER 28

Sitting down for lunch, Garon thought about what had happened to him before. Never in his wildest dreams would he have thought of touching a girl without her consent, let alone nearly kill her. So, he was naturally quite shocked when Clint told him of what had transpired in the fight between Karen and himself. The first thing he did, once he knew of it was go and apologise to Karen, who just smiled and said, "It's fine. As long as you don't kill me, we're cool."

Garon finished his lunch and went back to his room. As he sat down on his bed, he heard heavy footsteps coming down the corridor. He ignored it. But then, he heard grunting, as if there was an animal on the floor. He peeked out of the door, but saw no one there. He saw Ake and Dan walking towards him, and what was behind them.

The mysterious figure grabbed Dan and pushed Ake ahead, hoping to create a wide enough window of time to escape. By the time Garon and Ake could understand what had happened, the stalker had managed to climb up to the floor above a distance of three metres, with a now unconscious Dan over his shoulder. He was good, Garon thought, to climb up with a weight on his shoulder, literally. As they watched helplessly, the figure disappeared from their view.

Garn looked at Ake and said, "What are we going to tell Victoria?"

"For now, nothing."

"Want me to get Edmund? I can scout out within the walls of the city. If he has escaped, it can't be far. He will have to keep Dan unconscious if he wants to keep a low profile."

"How will he maintain a low profile if he walks around with a person on his shoulder?"

Something clicked in Garon's mind. "He won't be walking around. He would be using those transporters that our Trainers were talking about today."

"Then there is no way we can track him, even within the city walls."

Garon didn't like it, but he saw Victoria walking to them, and realised that he would have to create a cover story for Dan's absence. He hoped Ake was thinking on the same lines. Thankfully, Victoria went into her room. Garon and Ake then ran back to the field, where Reidan and Sens were talking among themselves. They blurted out the whole story, which the two Trainers listened to with rapt attention.

Sens spoke first, "Dan merges into an armoured Centaur, right?"

Reidan said, "No, that is Robert."

"I see. Did this kidnapper have any arm-guards?"

"I think so," Ake replied. "It was a Lion, if I am not wrong."

Reidan turned and asked Sens, "Could it be the Captain?"

"Maybe, but so many have been turned. It would be hard to tell. You boys better go back, we will take it from here. Don't breathe a word of this to anyone."

The two boys headed back and started talking to Emmanuel and Clint, neither of whom asked about Dan. Ake kept glancing at the sky, hoping Dan would drop out of the sky and give them some relief. Sadly, that did not happen. After an hour and a half of waiting, he got up and went straight to the throne room. He looked around for Lord Veryu, who wasn't there. He asked one of guards where their Guardians were being kept, and headed down that door. He looked around for Hadver, who jumped him from behind. He looked into Hadver's green eyes and said, "We got a job to do. You ready to go rogue?"

"Go rogue for what reason, exactly?" A voice behind him asked.

He spun around to see his sister, Hasha, standing in front of his only exit.

"I got to do something on my own. Let me go."

"No. Whatever reason you have to leave, it is not going to happen. We have to keep you in check, according to the Trainers. So, don't try any stunts."

Ake's shoulders slumped, clearly defeated. But what Hasha didn't see was the green flicker in his usually dark eyes. He took one step towards her, and jumped over her, onto the other side of the door, breaking the frame on his way out. Hadver ran behind him, and they bolted out of the throne room. Guards readied their weapons but Hadver made short work of them, and Ake burst out of the palace. He looked around for a way to escape and ran to the closest section of the city walls that he could find, only to find twenty guards hot on his tail. He knew he couldn't waste any time in fighting them. He neared the wall, which thankfully did not have a watchtower. He put his nails into the granite and managed to get some leverage. He was halfway up, when he saw that the reason no one was attacking him, was that the score of pursuers had only swords and no spears or bows and arrows. Hadver was running to the nearest gate, which was just open due to the passage of carts coming into the Capital. He got to the top, and saw that three guards were coming at him, from the nearest watchtower. He took a deep breath and jumped down. He hit the ground hard, but took off running into the forest ahead of him, Hadver by his side. They ran for half an hour, before Ake decided to stop. He knew that he was on his own now, and that he would have to find Dan fast.

Hadver suddenly started snarling at the trees ahead of them, though Ake couldn't hear anything. He decided that since he couldn't go back, he would make for Leonis, where he might find safety. From now, he had no friend except Hadver. He needed to head due north, for the border. With these thoughts in mind he started walking north. He remembered vaguely that he had a river to cross, after which there were no towns or cities. That river was one of the tributaries of the Fang River, the main river of Leonis. Until he crossed the last tributary, he would not be safe as it was a region of high erosion.

He heard the rush of running water soon after sunset. As it was still light, he managed to climb up a fallen tree to see what was ahead of him, and nearly lost his willpower.

Ahead of him was a river about twenty metres across, its bed lined with sharp rocks, some of which poked above the surface, like sharp teeth. The rocks Ake could just about see, so he had no idea what exactly was under the river surface. As if that was not enough, the river was actually ten feet below him and was rushing along fast enough to get him skewered by the protruding rocks. He climbed down the tree and looked at Hadver.

"Any ideas on how we are going to cross this hurdle?"

"I can help with that, if you want," came a familiar voice.

James appeared leaning on the nearest tree, his Raven on his forearm.

Ake smiled and said, "What are you doing out here?"

"Well, when I saw you walk to the throne room, I knew something was wrong, because we are not allowed to leave the palace. I decided to follow you once I saw you take your Guardian. What's his name, by the way?"

"Hadver. He is a Grey Wolf, the friendly version of an Ag-Wolf, which Garon has. What's your Guardian's name?"

"Riyo. He is a Mountain Raven. Now that we have got the formalities out of the way, I understand that you want a way across the river?"

"Yes. How are you going to help with that?"

"Watch me."

James closed his eyes and Riyo melted into his arm-guard. From his back, wings spread out. His fingers elongated and he kicked off his footwear. He asked Ake to pick them up for him. He first transferred Ake to the opposite bank and then went back for Hadver. As they set off on their way, Ake asked him, "Did you turn invisible to follow me out of the Capital?"

"Yes, I am the reason Hadver snarled after you guys stopped. I did not want you to think that the Trainers had sent me to capture you and bring you back."

It was getting dark fast and Ake was not worried that they were alone in the forest, subject to nature. He was actually worried that they were going to have trouble finding food. He looked at James, ahead of him, and thought of something.

"You have not asked me where I am going. Why?"

James stopped and said, "Two reasons. First, I know you are headed for Leonis. Second, even if I did not know where you were going, I trust you enough to follow you to the end of Lasgalan."

Ake looked up at the sky through the branches of the trees and said, "You know, you can fly us through the sky and save us a lot of time."

"I was thinking the same thing. But if I push Riyo to his limit, and I unmerge suddenly, we will both fall down on the trees, and get pierced by the branches, and then die. So it would be better if we walk for now."

There was a rustle in a bush ahead of them. Hadver charged into it. There was a cracking sound, and he emerged holding a deer in his mouth. Ake smiled and said, "Food problem solved."

CHAPTER 29

Chris charged into Garon's room, where he and Emmanuel were lying down in their beds, while Clint was reading a book.

"Where's James?"

Garon was the first one up. Looking around the room, he said, "And also, where is Ake?"

Within a minute, the four boys were out and started searching for a Trainer. They first bumped into Hasha, who told them of her brother's escape. Garon was now suspecting why Ake had gone rogue, but did not say anything. Just then, Lord Veryu appeared and listened to their entire story. She said that Ake and James would be found soon, if they had not crossed into any other District. She would send a message to the Lords of Leonis and Covis, informing them of the two escapees. She assured the five of them that the duo would not be harmed in any way.

Garon saw that she did not make any reference to Dan, who was missing. He decided that she probably knew about Dan, but did not want to shake anyone's morale any more than it was already.

Garon waited until she had gone, and then slipped out to the field. He needed to climb up the wall, and without

Edmund, it was going to be difficult. Somehow, he managed to get handholds no bigger than his palm, and used them to climb to the top. He glanced north and tried to use his binocular vision to locate Ake, if not Dan or James as well. He could not get a lock on any of them, or even Hadver. He needed to find them fast, so he tried to use his snake-like vision to get some heat from their bodies. Sadly, that also didn't work and all he got was a headache. He looked at no point in particular and said to the wind, "I hope you know what you are doing, Ake." He jumped down to the ground and went straight to Hasha's room. Seeing her in conversation with Karen and Victoria, he backed out of the door and turned, only to find himself face to face with the Ring bearer of Equis.

Garon tried to move out of her way, but she moved in the same way. Garon realised that she was not going to let him go. So, he started to talk.

"Hi. You are Adriana, right?"

"Yes. I want to know about Dan. Where exactly is he?"

Garon's mind went into overdrive, trying to think of a good excuse as to why no one would see Dan, Ake or James at dinner. But part of his mind was asking the question, "How does she know that Dan is missing?"

He could not thank Elesa enough for walking around to them and pulling Adriana away for a talk. He did not stay to ask what it was about, he bolted back to his room. He waited to be called for dinner, only then, did he step out of his room. But he realised that they had called them for dinner earlier than the normal time. The sun's light was still visible on the western horizon, though it was faint.

As they trooped into the dining room, it became evident that three people were missing. The Trainers walked in at the end of the meal and said, "We called you here earlier because we are going to have a little training exercise after this. You lot have half an hour to prepare. You can use weapons and armour from the armoury, which you will be shown. Your Guardians will be with you. But bear in mind, if you wear armour and then try to merge, the armour will be useless. It will disappear, but if you unmerge, it will be back on your bodies. Any questions?"

Adrian asked, "What kind of exercise is this?"

"Good question. It will be the Ring-bearers against the mergers."

Garon looked at Chris and Clint and wondered how they were going to fare, given that one of their own was missing. Nevertheless, he knew that they were strong fighters and got up. They first went to the armoury and grabbed their armours. The only one who did not was Robert. He went straight for his Guardian. Soon they reached the field where they had practised in the morning and saw that trees and shrubs were now present on the ground, as if to give this combat scenario a bit of a twist. Through the trees, Garon could see that the gate to the outside was also open.

Their Trainers came to them and said that the combat would end as soon as all the fighters on one side were captured. Once one person was captured, they could not escape or be freed. This placed the mergers at a huge advantage, since they were fifteen as opposed to the six Ring-bearers. As soon as they were given the signal, the mergers shot into the woods, merging at the same time. Elesa was the only one who could still utilise her Guardian, a Grey Wolf called Ketta. Garon went straight for the gate. He emerged out of the trees and saw that Elesa had also done the same. Chris came out at the same time, and for a minute the trio just stared at the woods, waiting for something to happen. Garon had an idea. He told Chris, "Why don't you try to disguise yourself as one of our opponents?"

"Good idea, Garon. But what if they are together? I will be captured instantly. Also I will have to curb Cronder's spirit to a great extent to get rid of my wings and talons."

Chris went back into the woods and first ran into Adrian, the Ring-bearer from Tauris. Knocking him unconscious with one hit, Chris dragged him back to where Garon and Elesa were waiting. He then unmerged and changed his form to match Adrian's. Since they couldn't get Chris to use the Ring of Tauris, Garon decided it was better that Chris should quietly take out the other Ring-bearers instead of coming into their plain view.

Chris crept back towards the field, where he thought the Ring-bearers had set up their base. He watched them through the trees, as one of the mergers was dragged out of the woods. Chris realised that somehow, Clint had been knocked out of the air and was now one of the twelve people captured by the five Ring-bearers. He knew that they wold only charge the remaining trio of mergers if they charged them together. Chris got an idea so foolhardy, his dad, who was all for recklessness, would tell him to back off from it. It wasn't that his dad was irresponsible; it was actually the contrary. His dad was the one who always pushing him to the edge, hoping to get the best out of Chris.

He walked out into the open and raised his hands. The five looked first at his hand to see if he was wearing the Ring, which of course, he was not. He hefted his mace and said, "Anyone here want broken bones?"

Then he proceeded towards them in his own sweet pace. The Ring-bearer of Equis opened her hand so that her palm faced the sky, and lifted her arm up. At the same time, the earth around Chris' legs rose up in two funnel-like projections, fastening onto them and even swings from the mace couldn't do anything to the earth. Adriana smiled and said, "Not all problems can be solved by violence, buddy."

"That is why we are here, isn't it?" Chris replied. There was a hint of humour in his voice. Thomas asked Hasha, "Can I have a bit of fun with him?"

Getting the approval, Thomas closed his fist and raised his hands. The earth on Chris' legs cracked and broke as he shot out of it. Thomas moved his hand in random directions, and Chris moved in the same way. The daylight had faded by now, and the only source of light was, as usual, the non-smoking torches on the walls. For some reason, Chris was smiling as he was being tossed around. Thomas asked him, "What's so funny?"

"You really think I would get caught like this, without any sort of backup?"

Chris reverted back to his original form and looked behind him. He shouted, "Cronder, a little help here please."

By the time Thomas understood what Chris really wanted, it was too late. Chris' shoes fell to the ground and he swooped down and caught Thomas by the shoulders. He flew back to his two friends, and saw that Adrian had woken up and was casually chatting with the duo. He laid Thomas down next to Elesa and said, "Take care of this one for me."

Garon said, "I will do this one, Clint. You and Elesa stay here. I have an idea. If this works and I pull it off without a problem, be happy. But if this works and I turn against you, knock me out cold without hesitation."

Elesa asked, "What are you planning on doing?"

"Wait and see."

Garon merged and felt Edmund trying to fight him, for control over his mind. This time, he did not hesitate. He let Edmund take control of his mind. But he made sure that he still had some control over his actions. He turned towards his four friends, who just nodded their heads. Garon turned to the woods and ran into them. The speed was incredible, more than what he had used when he was facing Karen. He stopped behind a tree, just out of sight of his opponents. He climbed up and peered through the branches. He could jump Hasha, who was the closest to the tree, but the moment he would hit the ground, Adriana would hold him to earth, ensuring that he would not be able to escape. He would need to take her out first. He leapt down and grabbed Hasha, one hand over her mouth.

He disappeared behind the tree line before anyone could notice, or so he thought. Vesper had seen him take away Hasha, and started after him. She chased him and sent a wave of fire after him. It stung, but did not irritate him as such. He burst out of the woods, Vesper in pursuit. He calmly set Hasha down on the ground and faced Vesper, who realised that she was outnumbered four to one. She summoned some fire from her Ring and held a ball of it in her hands. The only one who could even get close to her would be Chris, though his wings would get burned. He flapped his wings twice and the strong wind extinguished Vesper's flames. But she just created it again. Elesa's Wolf had evidently had enough. She leapt at Vesper, causing a momentary distraction, while Garon and Chris calmly captured her and put her with the other two.

Chris stretched his wings and said, "Three down, three to go."

Elesa said, "Let me go this time. I have a higher chance of not getting caught than you two twits."

"Now that is just rude, Elesa. You cannot call us twits unless we really are twits."

"Well, boys will be boys."

"Hey, it is in our nature to be charming." Chris winked at her.

Garon looked out towards the mountains in the distance. They would have been faint for anyone else, but not Garon. He thought about how easy it would be to sneak out of the city at this hour, head for the mountains and not be seen again. Just then, he heard a twig snap as someone walked out of the woods. He felt the earth under his legs shift and could not move his feet. Adriana and Patrick emerged, the Rhodonite Ring on Adriana's finger glowing faintly. Chris immediately flew up and stayed out of Adriana's range. Patrick glanced up at him and said, "You have to come back down sooner or later, and when you do, you will be captured."

Chris watched as his two partners were taken through the woods and came out the other side. They were placed with the others, all of whom looked up at Chris as if he were their last hope, which in a way, he was. He swooped down and landed on a branch of a tree taller than most others. At that moment, Patrick unleashed a new weapon.

A fire tornado came right at Chris, who shot into the sky. The tornado kept swirling and Patrick manipulated it to rise higher and higher. But it was taking a great deal of his concentration, Chris could see. He waited for an opening and struck. He shot through the tornado, covering himself with his wings, like a cocoon. He came out of the tornado, knocking out Patrick in the process. Picking him up, Chris spread his wings and flew up a few metres, when he felt something hold his legs. Adriana was pulling his leg, literally. After a minute of struggling, Cronder could not contribute any more energy.

Chris felt his strength fail and would have fallen hard on the ground, if not for Adriana's quick thinking. She levelled him gently down, using his legs as a pivot. Clint, seeing that the exercise was over, flew over to the other side to get the others. As all of them walked into the Palace, their Trainers met them and asked them to unmerge and hand over the Rings. Garon was quite shocked to see that Adrian's Ring came off easily. He was then told that unless the Ring was given out of the wielder's own will, it was not possible to remove it.

They went into their rooms and till late in the night Chris and Garon could not get any sleep. They only went to sleep an hour after midnight, and that too, into fitful sleeps.

CHAPTER 30

James and Ake crossed the border between Leonis and Talis at around midnight. Since they were both very tired, they sat down on the ground, while Riyo flew to the nearest branch and went to sleep. Hadver made a small circle around them and lay down close to them, so that he could protect them in case someone attacked them. Within a minute, even he was asleep, though Ake was sure that his nose and ears were still on alert. James said, "You know, it is a bit difficult for someone to earn my respect, but you have done it. To leave the safety of a city and your friends, risking your life to try and find a friend, that decision takes a lot of willpower to make."

"Thanks. But you are the one who took more of a risk, following me here. And you did it without a second thought."

James said, "I never really say this, but I personal feel that it takes the strongest willpowers to make the toughest decisions."

"Can you stop with the philosophy, please? There is only so much I can take in one day."

"Well, I guess we should get some sleep. Getting across the border wall was a bit risky."

"A bit? Speak for yourself. You can turn invisible with just a thought. I have to hear for threats. If my ears fail me and I get caught, even you will not be able to save me."

"Hmm. Goodnight."

"Goodnight."

The duo woke up an hour after sunrise, stretched themselves and continued through the District. They reached a cliff top and looked across the tops of the trees that they still had to cross to get to the nearest city.

Ake turned to James and said, "I don't think you would mind flying me across now, would you?"

"It is not you that I am worried about, it is Hadver. I can fly you across, no problem. Hadver can follow us from the ground, but if something happens to him, we may not be able to know where he is."

Ake looked around and sighed. Leaving Hadver back in Logder for the Games at Shodor was bad for him, but now hearing that there was a chance of him never seeing Hadver again, was gut-wrenching. He made a decision.

"James, you go back. Tell them that you tried to stop me, but I did not listen. I will continue on my journey for answers."

"Look Ake..."

"You said that you trust me. Now is the time to practise what you preach. So please, go back James, I have to do this on my own."

Ake suddenly pushed James off the cliff, Riyo diving down after him. The full fall down the cliff was two hundred metres, which would have been a hard hit for James' skeleton. But Riyo merged with him not even halfway down and, spreading his wings, James flew back up to the cliff top. Neither Ake nor

Hadver were present there. James had not seen them come down, so he deduced that they had gone back the way they had come. But he could see nothing in that direction. He decided to go to the city that he could see in the distance. The first thing that he would need was a bag for his shoes. He flew to the edge of the city and unmerged. He walked up to the gates and shouted at one of the guards on the wall to open it. After telling the guard who he was, James was allowed through the gates. He knew that he was not near the Capital, and asked for a place to stay.

One of the guards let him come to his house and gave him some water. They chatted and the guard, whose name was Esdah, asked him why he had come to Leonis. James thought carefully and said, "I came here for a vacation. I was hiking in the mountains near the head of the river. Then it went black till I woke up, washed ashore near here. I saw this town and here I am."

Esdah seemed to buy his story and said, "Feel free to stay here for some more time. I am the only one living in the house."

"No other family?"

"No. My parents died last year, my brother disappeared a few years back, and I am unmarried."

"Sorry to hear that."

"Don't be. I never wanted to get married. Can you imagine raising a child in an environment where it can be picked upon? I would not have kids and serve my District, rather than have kids and have them live in fear that I would not be returning at any point in their lives."

"Why not leave the army and then get married?"

"Sadly, each District's armies have their own laws. Here, in Leonis, once you join the army, you only leave it the day you die."

"Oh, I see. How long have you been in the army?"

"Long enough to have nightmares about everyone I have killed or put into jail."

"In layman's terms?"

"About ten years."

"And your brother?"

"Raze was a carefree person. He spoke only when spoken to. He would rather spend his day in nature's hands, than in a city. Our father wanted both of us to join the army, but Raze said that he wanted to have a family of his own, not a life where he could die anytime. Sometimes, I feel that he made the right choice by not wanting to join the army."

"Do you think that he is still alive, somewhere in Lasgalan?"

"There comes a time when you have to let go of hope, hope that you knew was false from its beginning."

"Never give up hope, no matter how small. Some hope is better than no hope at all, even if it is false." James felt strange giving advice to someone who was more than twice his age.

"That same hope was what ate away at my soul for the first five years of Raze's disappearance. I have learnt the hard way to let go of hope."

"Surely you don't give up on family?"

"You remind me of myself, James. Me, once upon a time. Naïve, innocent of the ways of the world. You wait till your time come to make a sacrifice, one that will eat away at your conscience all your life. Trust me, that day is coming."

James did not like the certainty with which Esdah spoke.

Esdah continued, "I have something I would like to give you. Promise me that you will not part with it."

"Okay, what is it?"

"A potion that can bring anyone back from the dead. It is made from the Sapphire Rose from Logder."

"When did you visit Logder?"

"A long time ago."

James looked at the tube that Esdah had given him. It was an inky shade of blue and looked solid, until James shook it. Riyo pecked at the tube, after which he turned away from it.

"Animals cannot stand the smell of this potion. For them, it is bad. You can't bring them back from the dead with this potion." Esdah explained.

"Thanks. If it is not too much to ask for, can I have a bag for my shoes?"

"Sure. Just wait here."

Esdah came back with a brown bag big enough for two pairs of shoes. When James looked into it, he saw one pair of shoes, too big for him, but it would fit him when he would merge with Riyo. He smiled at Esdah and said, "Thanks, but I need only the bag, not the shoes."

"Keep both. You can use the shoes when you and your Guardian merge."

CHAPTER 31

James stared in shock at Esdah. But he regained his composure and said, "What do you mean, Guardian?"

"Don't try to play funny with me. Do you who I am exactly?"

"Well, no."

"Then let me break it down for you. I am Esdah, God of the Underworld. I oversee every soul, human, plant, animal and all sentient beings on Lasgalan and other lands."

"You mean that there are other places apart from Lasgalan, beyond the seas?"

"Obviously. But I don't think that you will be going to them anytime soon, given the path that you are on is a different one."

James was getting nervous at the rate with which Esdah was casually talking about all that James knew. He started sweating. Riyo perched on James' shoulder and cawed loudly at Esdah, as if he had caught onto James' emotions. James wondered how long it would take him to merge and fly out of the city before Esdah could stop him.

Esdah laughed and said, "Don't even think about flying away. I will catch you before you can fly off."

James needed an exit route, and fast. One option was to fight this self-proclaimed God, the other was to shout and scream for help. He was armed only with two knives. Esdah on the other hand, had a sword next to him. The only advantage that James had was that, in close quarters, the sword was pretty much useless, whereas the knives required a short distance to wield.

He tried to stall.

"So, am I a hostage here, or can I go?"

"Neither. You can stay here, but you can't leave."

"Well, I can actually."

"Prove it."

The next moment, Esdah found a knife impaled in his abdomen. Looking back up at James, he said, "Do you really think that a knife..."

James kicked him in the face, dazing him for a second. He merged with Riyo, kicked down the door, and flew up into the sky. He shot past the city walls high enough for them not to notice him, and headed away, with no particular direction in mind. His first priority was to get food for Riyo and himself, so once he felt he was far enough from Esdah, he set himself down and scored some deer. He did not unmerge, but hoped that some of the nutrition from the animal also went to his Guardian. He heard voices suddenly and climbed up a tree to investigate. He couldn't see much, so he did not bother to search for the source of those voices. He stretched his wings and took off from the branch.

He circled the same spot a few times, gaining a height of about hundred metres before gliding west. He was nowhere close to getting his answers. Ake had told him about Dan and their conversation with the Trainers. James knew that he could not find Ake in such a huge District. He did not even know the way which Ake had gone in. His only two options were to get to Leonis' Capital and get information from there, or go back to Talis and grill their Trainers for information. He thought for a moment, and then changed his direction to south. It would take him a day to get back, at the very least, so he decided to make his first stop in Talis, at whichever town he passed first. He had the entire afternoon and evening to fly, so he thought, "I will take a stop only at evening. My lunch is taken care of."

Just after crossing into Talis, which was just past dusk, James landed on solid land. There, his head swam and Riyo unmerged from him. The bird lay on its side and closed its eyes, absolutely exhausted. James felt a pang of guilt and cradled Riyo in his arms. He then had an idea. He took the bag that Esdah had given him, removed the shoes, and placed Riyo inside. The bag was not smelling, so James was happy. He hung the bag from one of his knife sheaths, the one which was now empty, and walked on. He came to the first town around dinner time. Here, the gate was just closing for the night, so he was allowed in. He asked for a place to eat and sleep, and was directed to the nearest pub. He didn't have any money with him, save one silver coin that he always carried around for emergencies. He gave it to the owner of the pub, who gave him a room at the back, with food and water. Riyo too got something to eat. He finished his food and was soon fast asleep. James was speaking to the owner for some time after that. The owner seemed friendly enough, but then again, so had Esdah. James did not let his guard down the entire conversation, and later went to sleep himself. His last though before sleeping was, "I wonder what Ake is doing now, with only Hadver for company."

The only reason he was alone was because he was afraid that Hadver might get hurt trying to get to that town, where he and Ake were supposed to go together. He wondered how much it would hurt him if Riyo died, but decided not to think about it.

CHAPTER 32

Gonth woke up the next morning at sunrise, as was his daily routine since childhood, though he often went back to sleep after that. He looked out at the lightening sky and walked out of the room. It was a bit chilly, and the guards were talking among themselves. How they could stay up all night and bear the cold, Gonth did not know. Nevertheless, he respected them for keeping watch over them, people who they did not even know.

He glanced north, and could just about see the tributary of the Fang River through the light fog. There was something black moving in the fog too, though it was too small and far away for him to see what it was. As it got closer, Gonth understood what it was. He watched James approach and land ten feet from him. Since only the two of them were awake at that time, James did not want to wake the others. He unmerged, went to keep Riyo with the other Guardians, came back to Gonth and the duo talked for a bit. One of the guards went to inform the Trainers of James' return. The others woke up slowly, met James, and all of them went for breakfast. There, Sens asked James where he had been for nearly two days. James saw no problem in telling them the truth. When he finished, he turned to Hasha and said, "I am sorry that I was ready to follow your brother and not bring him back. His disappearance is on me."

Hasha said, "I do not blame you. I would have not done the same thing, but since you and I are two different people to him, I cannot say much. I wold have preferred that you bring him back to me, though." The last sentence was said with a bit of humour and a wink to James.

James turned to their Trainers, who were in discussion among themselves. He needed answers, so he did not beat around the bush, he went straight for the point.

"What are you not telling us? Ever since I mentioned Esdah, it seems as if I have made things worse for you. Would you mind telling us everything we ought to know?"

Reidan sighed and said, "Well, you guys should know this much. Finish your breakfast and follow me. The others maybe more old-school and conservative, but I sure am not. I will tell you everything. We owe you this much."

James felt sad that he had to force his opinion onto people who were older than him, but it had to be done. All of them filed out of the room, through a door in the wall of the dining room itself. As they walked in, they saw that they were on a balcony of a huge library. They were on the second level, as they could see the ground level below them. There were five levels to the library and the main reading area was below them. Reidan led them down there. Once they were settled, Reidan said, "This library contains every bit of Lasgalan's history. Any question that you have, you can come down here and ask aloud. Within a minute, the relevant book will be placed on your table. Here, let me demonstrate."

Reidan sat down a table and said, "Who is Esdah?"

He did not raise his voice, but the library appeared to have heard him. There was a sound of rushing wind, even though the windows on the walls were closed. A thin, paper-back book titled "GODS OF LASGALAN" appeared in front of him. On the first page was a picture of a smoky being, about ten feet in height, wielding a sword as dark as himself, but only half his height. He sported dark wings and seemed to be wreathed in flames. His eyes were actual flames, bright orange in colour.

Reidan held it up for everyone to see. He asked James, "Was this who you met?"

"No, he seemed human enough."

"Then what you saw was only a small manifestation of his power. If he does not send out a manifestation of himself, this is what he would look like. You would not die looking at this, his true form, but you would not be able to comprehend what you are seeing, no matter how strong and advanced your mind is. Your mind would simply snap."

"How many gods are there that we need to know of?"

"Only two that are of importance at this point. One is Esdah, God of the Underworld. The other is Ara, Goddess of ice. They are the type who will only help you if you can show that you are worth helping."

"Well that maybe all well and good, but how are we supposed to fight the war that you want us to?" Gonth spoke up. Next to him, Vincent and Patrick nodded, approving his question.

Reidan closed the book and said, "Very well. You already know that two people are missing. Ake you know about. Dan was kidnapped by one of Yedgal's men."

Clint interrupted, "I know this is completely out of context and maybe a bit far-fetched, but hear me out. Yedgal's men knocked out the Wolf Tribe years ago. The "War of the Tribes" as you so put it, starts from that time as well. Is it not possible that at least some people survived?"

"Oh, some people did survive. Three, to be exact. They are Ake, Elesa and Garon."

"Ok. What I am saying is, is it not possible to get the Tribes to stop warring with each other and focus on beating back Yedgal's forces before they decide to make Lasgalan a bad place to live in?"

"No. You will have to beat Yedgal's forces first. Once that is accomplished, only then will the Tribes listen to you and stop their constant warring. Sadly, there is no other way."

James thought of something and asked, "If this was just a small manifestation of Esdah, how would he have managed to keep himself hidden in plain sight?"

Reidan replied, "He would have appeared as the couple's first child, stayed with them for so many years, making everyone believe that he was always there. It is not that difficult."

Jacob asked, "Is there anything else we should know other than Gods walking among us?"

"Yes."

Reidan got up and threw the book up. It got whisked up somewhere on the fourth level. Reidan then called out, "Monsters of Lasgalan."

A huge book appeared on each of the six tables, including one in Reidan's hand. He opened it and said, "Everyone open to page fifty."

The heading was "Land Monsters".

The first one they saw was called a Battos. Karen looked at the creature, which seemed to be a copy of her, including the blue flames coming out of its nose. The Battos seemed to have a weakness that was water. It seemed appropriate enough, then, for it to only breed on the mountain slopes. It ate anything that came its way, from small birds and insects, to Bulls and Wolves. It ate berries and plants as well. It had impenetrable skin, could keep its footing in any situation if it was not dazed, and got huge boosts of power from lightning strikes. To defeat it, Reidan said, one would need more than just brute force. Battois (plural of a Battos) weighed in at around hundred and fifty kilograms, but could also be two hundred kilograms. The flames coming out of the nose of a Battos could disintegrate even the toughest armour into ash.

The next one they saw was a Constry. It was four-armed, bipedal creature that could use each hand to fight four different people at the same time. It had a small bump running across the head from front to back. That was supposed to be the Constry's brain. It had a weakness to birch and yew wood. One touch of either of these woods meant a five-day coma for the creature, during which time it could be killed. It could regenerate almost every body part cut off from it, only if there was one mutilated part of his body. Its head could not be regenerated. Its skin, however was not impenetrable.

Reidan snapped his fingers once everyone was done reading about the two monsters. The books were then taken somewhere on the third level.

"Everyone out. We need to commence weapon training now. No Guardians, only weapons."

And all of them went out to the field. Each one had their own weapon and formed a circle. They were to stay in their District groups, which meant that the Wolves and the Horses were one person short each. Gonth, Emmanuel, Karen and Adrian were probably the most intimidating people but they were not the most challenging. That title went to Dan's group. Isabella, Dan, Emmanuel and Adriana looked the fiercest. They were raring to go. With their varied fighting styles, they would be the hardest people to get out. Edward burst into flames, but Reidan called out, "No powers, only weapons."

Edward argued, "But Trest has no control over her powers. She will survive no matter what happens."

"I see nothing wrong with that."

James pointed at Garon and said, "You are mine and mine alone."

It seemed as if everyone was singling out their opponents. Chris hefted his mace and pointed it at Emmanuel, who, in return, pointed his club at him. Patrick and Vesper used their Rings to form fiery whips, which they cracked on the ground, just to make a statement of their power. Hasha used her Ring to a sword made out of ice. When she touched the tip to the ground, ice started to creep out onto the surrounding ground, though a bit slowly. Thomas elevated a few feet of the ground and turned his palms upwards. Two miniature tornadoes appeared and swirled fast in his hands. Adriana and Adrian closed their fists and raised them upwards. From either side of them, two fists erupted from the ground and mimicked their movements. Their message was clear. Anyone trying to get close to them would get beaten back severely.

Reidan shouted, "You cannot immobilise anyone and then fight them. You must fight them and then subdue them. Begin!"

The selected opponents charged towards each other. The others just charged anyone who was not of their District. The two most impressive duelling pairs, were without a doubt, Garon and James, and Vincent and Clint.

Garon and James took close-quarter fighting to whole new level as they slashed, dived and parried each other's attacks. The grace with which they fought was something Reidan had not seen in a long time. To use such sharp and small weapons, one needed to be very good with their hand-eye coordination. These two youths definitely had it in them. Their agility and flexibility was good, though Reidan was sure that it was nothing compared to what they would be needing when attacking Yedgal's forces. That would be whole different level of fighting.

Vincent and Clint were equally matched in terms of speed and strength. But Reidan could see that Clint had an advantage with his extra five inches of height and army training. He may have been lighter than Vincent, but that did not stop him. His spear suddenly became a trident and caught Vincent's javelin just below the tip. He turned the trident sharply in Vincent's direction, snapping the tip in the process. Vincent looked at his javelin, but for some reason smiled. He threw down the wooden rod and made a lunge for the trident, grabbing the two extreme points. Clint said, "Release your fingers, or they will become mangled when I close the trident."

"I see no harm happening to me if you do that."

Clint did not see why Vincent could be so arrogant, so he closed the trident. Then, the impossible happened. As the points collapsed back to centre, so did Vincent's fingers. On making contact with the centre point, Vincent's fingers did not break. However, the other two points snapped at their joints. Vincent opened his palms which did not appear to have any visible damage done to them. The other two points of Clint's trident were also in his palms.

But something inside Clint had also snapped. He dropped to his knees and allowed Vincent to take him out of the fight. As Reidan watched, he thought he saw Clint crying.

CHAPTER 33

Ake dried his eyes as the rain stopped. He stared out of the cave that Hadver and he had taken up residence on to avoid the storm that had been raging outside. They had had a good run to get away from James, but even they had to stop for a break. As the storm clouds cleared, the full moon shone brightly like a guiding light for the duo. Ever since leaving James, they had covered about five leagues, most of it walking. They had stopped at sunset and managed to get delicious rabbit to feast on. Ake hoped that it would sustain them for a few hours, since he was planning on merging and continuing onto the Capital of Leonis. He hoped to get there by the evening of the next day. Once he was sure that it was not raining, he stood up and walked to the entrance of the cave and said, "Whenever you are ready, Hadver."

Hadver growled softly. Ake felt his presence on his own mind. He thought, "Wherever you are, Dan, I will find you."

With these thoughts in mind, Ake took a step back and bolted out of the cave. He extended his nails and grabbed the opposite wall of the canyon that he was in. He could see the Fang River tributary a hundred feet below him. He let go from the wall and dropped down about ten feet. Hadver dropped down next to him, balancing himself on a ledge no wider than four inches.

Ake rolled his eyes and said, "Show-off."

They continued like that till they reached the floor of the canyon. Then they started walking in the direction of the flow of the Fang. Ake heard a splash ahead of them, as if something had fallen into the river. Hadver and he charged ahead at full speed, Hadver leading him to wherever his nose guided him. They reached a small fork in the river, where Hadver stopped, sniffing the air. He turned a full circle and looked up the moon. He let out a loud howl that echoed across the canyon. Ake understood that Hadver was upset at not being able to track whatever it was. It had to be either an animal or a human, otherwise Hadver would not have run so fast. Ake looked up at the walls of the canyon that seemed to be slopping down, in the direction of the flow of the river. They continued their walk and saw the torches of a town in the distance. It was about a league away, which, in Hadver's pace, was three minutes. However, the main problem was right in front of them.

The river dropped down as a waterfall for some distance. Ake could hear the water hit the bottom, but could not estimate the distance between them and the ground below. His only way of getting down was by clawing his way down the rock face. He would survive, but Hadver would not be able to get a grip on the slippery surface. He turned back and saw a figure in their path. Hadver did not move a muscle, nor did he growl. He sat on his haunches, as if awaiting a command. Ake did not want to wait for the figure to start issuing commands, so he said, "Hadver, do me a favour and crush this guy's neck bones."

Hadver did not budge. Instead, he whimpered a bit and stayed put. Ake did not like this. He did not even have an axe to defend himself with. He tried to stall a bit, so he started speaking.

"Who are you? What do you want with us?"

"Do you not know who I am? Then again, I can't blame you. You have been through so much ever since I last saw you."

"Dad?"

"Dad is a general term. I honestly prefer the term "father"."

Ake felt as if he was being pulled apart layer by layer. He struggled to form a complete sentence.

"But how? I thought..."

"Oh, I am very much dead. This is my spirit talking to you. I am not really here."

"I-I have so many questions. I kept quiet so long."

"I know you do. You have always felt out of place. But remember this, you are never in the wrong place. It maybe that you are in the right place at the wrong time. Never the other way around."

"Yeah, that would be weird."

"I wish I could touch you son. It has been so long, if not too long. Hadver, how are you doing?"

Hadver only whimpered, but he got up and walked towards the figure. He passed right through him.

"Hadver, it is only an apparition, you cannot feel him." Ake then noticed something about his father's apparition.

"How come I can only see your outline, but not your face or body?"

"I chose to appear to you as this. You do not need to see my face, you only need to hear my voice. I will guide you. All you need to do is ask."

"What is your name?"

"That also you need not know. Just know this, Garon is your brother."

"What?"

But by then, the apparition had faded away.

Hadver paced up and down where Ake's father had been. He came back to Ake and licked his hand, as if trying to bring Ake back to his senses. But Ake did not move. Everything he had brought himself to be in fourteen years, gone in a conversation of less than five minutes. The flow of the Fang was not very strong, enough to keep the duo walking upstream again without hindrance, but Ake could have been washed off the cliff, just because he was not himself. Now, he could understand the similarity between Garon and himself. But then, what did that make Elesa in relation to him? He did not want to dwell on that, so he changed his thoughts to Hasha. He thought about how she would have felt about him running off. If James was not dead, he would have had the common sense to fly back to Talis and tell the others about what was happening. Ake knew that he had taken a risk by pushing James off that cliff, but he was betting that Riyo would have gone after him. If Riyo had not managed to get to James, then Ake had inadvertently sacrificed a good fighter of the Talons.

For all Ake was, there were many flaws in him. One of them was, if he ventured for too long on a thought, he would start to lose focus in his surroundings. This time, also, he became too unfocused. He did not hear the close growl, nor did he hear the source of the growl jump from the cliff above him.

Hadver saved Ake. He could smell the new animal, and leapt in its path before it could tackle Ake. Both beasts immediately regained their footing and circled each other. Ake could not see the other animal clearly. All he could tell was that it was slightly smaller than Hadver and that it had two-toned eyes. One eye was yellow and the other was silver. Hadver stood protectively in front of Ake, forcing the other animal back towards the edge of the cliff. It snapped in warning to Hadver, and then bounded towards the wall it had jumped down from. Its paws seemed to stick to the rock-face as it climbed up. It glanced back at them, but Hadver sent it off with two strong barks.

Ake smiled, knowing that Hadver could handle anything, but realised something was wrong. Hadver was shuddering. As he looked closer, he saw that Hadver was bleeding on his right side, near his shoulder. Ake knelt down next to him and said, "Hang in there, buddy. I will get you to safety."

Ake actually had no idea how to get Hadver to safety. He just needed to keep Hadver alive, till they reached that town. The problem was, Hadver and Ake had merged, so Ake could feel Hadver's emotions in his mind as well. He could not concentrate well, but steeled his resolve to save his Guardian. He was not going to let Hadver die so soon.

He picked up the two-hundred-pound Wolf and slung him over his shoulder. He walked to the edge of the cliff. He still could not see the bottom of the waterfall, but decided to leave it in the hands of fate. Placing one hand on the ground to steady himself, he drew in a deep breath and jumped down.

CHAPTER 34

D an woke up, only to find himself tied and gagged. He could not see anything, so he guessed that his captor had placed a cloth over his eyes as well. He could tell that wherever he was, it had steps. He was slung onto his captor's shoulder and heard his footsteps echoing across the place he was walking on. It sounded as if they were walking on marble. This meant that they were somewhere up in the mountain range of Lasgalan, the Dividing Mountains. They were so called since they divided Lasgalan in two halves, with three Districts on each side. On the east side were Equis, Logder and Tauris. On the west were Leonis, Talis and Covis. The range continued north, becoming the Rhodonite Hills of Equis.

He heard his captor grunt as he climbed the last step and set Dan down on the cold floor. Dan heard a deep voice ask, "Did you succced?"

Another voice, which Dan assumed was his captor's, said, "I have got him. He offered little resistance."

"Did anyone see you?"

"No. I managed to get him alone."

"I understand that you had second thoughts on wanting to go through with this."

"It matters not now. I have already got him."

"Remove the cloth from his eyes."

The cloth was removed, but it did not really help Dan's vision. He was seeing everything out of focus. He registered that he was facing a man sitting on a small flight of steps, like Lord Veryu's throne room. Behind him was some object that was covered in a black cloth. The man sitting on the steps was dark, short and muscular. He was wearing nothing extravagant, just a plain pant. On his chest was a type of armour that Dan had never seen before. From what he could make out, it consisted of two black straps that ran diagonally across his chest, forming an X, connected by a metal piece in the middle. On either side of the man, two metal pieces were fixed between the straps. The upper part and lower part of the X had no metal piece, making the man vulnerable to attacks at those two places. He had a beard that was completely white, contrasting with his complexion. He carried no weapons, but Dan was sure that he had one hidden behind him.

"How much of the drug did you use?"

"Only half the bottle."

"That is a lot. He will not be able to focus properly for another twelve hours, at the very least. Take him to the lock up and keep a double guard on him. Once he is ready, we can use him."

"Very well, my Lord."

This puzzled Dan. Just now the dark man had been addressed as a Lord. But before that, the two men were talking quite informally. As he was picked up again, the dark man called out, "By the way, Raze."

His captor stopped and turned around.

"Yes, my Lord?"

"Once King Yedgal is revived, you will be rewarded with a District of your own to rule as you will."

"Thank you. If I may, I would like to rule over Leonis."

"We will see what King Yedgal says once he is revived. Till then, keep up the good work."

Dan kept his eyes shut till he felt Raze put him on the ground again. He felt his gag getting removed and his hands were also untied. He heard a metal door close and lock. He waited until he could not hear Raze's footsteps anymore. He then opened his eyes. His vision was still out of focus, but at least he could move his hands. He felt for a wall and sat up against it. His breathing became steady and he stopped shaking. The cell was not cold, but there was an occasional draught coming into it. He tried to piece together where he was and how he would have to escape from the place.

The cell itself seemed to be a hole carved into the earth. There was no reinforcement on the ceiling, nor on the sides. The earth felt a bit moist at the back of the cell, as if there was water behind it. However, the other sides of the cell were dry and hard. The only exit was from the door, which was basically iron bars in a rectangular frame. The lock however, was not iron. It looked like an alloy of iron and some other metal. Dan crawled to the door and pulled himself up, using the bars of the door as a support. He slipped his hand through the bars and touched the lock. Immediately, he felt his hand burn, as if he had touched an acid. He withdrew his hand from the lock and understood what the other component of the lock was.

"Mercury. Why mercury, of all things?" Dan asked aloud.

One of his guards said, "We know who you guys are, and what your gifts are. So, we place you in cells where your powers become your bane. You can't go berserk and punch your way out of this. The cell will collapse if you try to punch your way out of it. If you try to break the lock, well, you saw what happened with just one touch. Imagine if you tried to punch it multiple times."

Dan slid back down to the ground and crawled back to his place. He did not know how long he had been unconscious, but he knew that he needed to eat soon, otherwise his high metabolism would get the better of him, and kill him.

Just then, someone slipped a plate of ham and vegetables into his cell. The smell of food got Dan into a trance and he crawled to the food. He finished in five minutes and felt much better. His vision still had not cleared, but it was starting to. He managed to stand up without any support. This gave him a bit of hope. He slid the plate back to the door, where it vanished. Dan wondered how he was going to survive in this place. He punched the back wall, because it was softer and would be easier to manipulate. His hand came out of the wall, cut in five different places. He saw that the wounds were not deep, but as it was, he could not feel pain. Looking at the wall closely, he saw that it was filled with small, sharp stones. Some of the stones had crumbled where he contacted them with his metal coated bones.

He had no bow with him, but his spare arrowhead was there. For how long he would get any use out of it was the question. He took it out and started to pry out stones from the wall, only in one spot. He relied more on feel than on his eyesight, since he could only see distorted images. Once he cleared out sufficient space, he turned back to make sure the guards were not watching, and punched the wall again. He managed to get an inch of mud away from the centre, but he had to once again start prying stones from the wall. This went on for some time. At the end of half an hour, he had not even got six inches of mud out. The stones were now tightly packed and it was difficult to get the arrowhead between them. Exhausted, Dan set his arrowhead down and lay down on the ground. He wondered how Frea was feeling. After all, the Talons would have made his friends use their Guardians, and Frea would have wondered why he had not come. Dan tried to think of the first time Frea had saved him. Frea had thrown himself in front of Dan, to save him from a meteor strike. The meteor had left a nasty wound on Frea's side. His blue skin, after that, had a thin line of red across his ribcage.

Dan closed his eyes and tried to convince himself that somebody was coming to rescue him. However, he knew that if they ran into Xristos, they would be fighting for their lives. They might not be walking away from that fight alive. The only way he could escape his cell was through the door, but first he was going to have to break the lock. The bars on the door were alright to touch, but Dan had no idea how much power it would take to get the bars to bend, let alone break. He also had to wait for the guards to go away before he tried any stunt with the door. The only source of light in his cell was a torch. There was a constant vibration below Dan and he could feel it through the floor.

He decided to try and sense the emotions of the guards outside, but he got nothing. Like he had been told, the cell had been designed to stop him from using his powers. He could have appealed to the emotions of the guards, maybe get them to his side and escaped. But he could not. His vision cleared finally and he was able to see without second guessing himself. He peeked outside and saw that the guards were talking among themselves. He saw someone coming towards the cell. The guards too noticed him and snapped to attention. The new person waved his hand and said, "I will be speaking to the prisoner alone, no need to be so wound up."

The guards relaxed. The man put his face near the bars and looked Dan straight in the eyes. Dan stared right back at him. He wondered how long it would take him to plunge the arrowhead into the man's chest, so he moved closer to the door to minimize that time.

The man started off, "I am Raze. I captured you and brought you here. You are the first in a short list of Chosen Ones to be brought here. You will be used to bring back King Yedgal and in doing so, will help bring Lasgalan to its Golden Age."

"If you want my help, you will have to use my cold dead body."

"That is sort of the plan. We will first prepare your body for the soul transfer. If you survive, all well and good. If you do not, however, it does not matter. Your soul is required, not your body or blood."

Dan was seriously considering plunging his arrowhead into Raze's stomach. Maybe if he did that, he could coerce the guards to open the gate and let him escape. Before he could think of doing it, he decided to play smart. He asked, "Do you need one from each District to do the transfer?"

Raze laughed and said, "No. we just need six. They can be from two Districts; it would not matter. We just need six, preferably the stronger ones."

Dan understood what Raze was saying. They were looking for six of the Chosen Ones whose gifts would help each other, rather than hinder each other. Dan had one of the most powerful gifts out of the eighteen Chosen Ones, but he saw that Raze was talking about those whose merging was stronger than the others'. He needed to get out fast, but Raze had no intention of letting him go, apparently.

"So, you think you are some big shot, who can walk around and get people to do your bidding?"

Dan understood that Raze was playing on his ego, and fortunately for Dan, he had a small one. He calmly stared at Raze as the latter kept trying to play on his ego. Raze stopped when he realised that Dan was doing nothing.

"Who are you?"

"My name is Dan of Equis, and I will not be bullied by a coward."

Raze looked in shock at Dan. He spoke softly, "Xristos will have my heart for this blunder."

Dan decided that this was his chance to taunt Raze. "What happened, mister high and mighty? Got the wrong person, I see. Who did you have to take?"

"Robert. I needed an Equine called Robert."

"Well, explain this to Xristos now. I want to know what he says to you."

"Still, you will suffice." Raze looked up with a smile. "Your gift is a rarity. Maybe I will be forgiven."

So saying, Raze winked at Dan, as if they had shared a joke. He turned and walked back the way he had come. Dan could not believe his bad luck. He had started to hope that he may be let out from this prison, only to be told that he was sufficient for whatever they were going to do with his soul. In anger he punched one of the bars of the door. It did not break, but it let Dan get some anger out of his system. He tried to strike up a conversation with the guards, but the might as well have been talking to a wall for all the response he got. He thought of plunging the arrowhead into his chest, but thought the better of it. He stood a better chance of staying alive and fighting his way out, than being dead and subjecting himself to Xristos, Raze and whatever sick operation they were going to do on him.

He knew that it was going to be night soon, since he could feel his eyes getting heavy and he felt too exhausted to do anything else, so he closed his eyes and went to sleep.

ABOUT THE AUTHOR

The author, Darius C. Modi, is (at the time of writing) a college student from Kolkata, India, who loves fiction and is an avid reader. His main inspiration for the series was The Lord of the Rings and The Hobbit Trilogies. He grew up fascinated by European mythologies, particularly Greek, Roman, Norse and also liked Egyptian mythology.

He likes movies and is not afraid to push his writing to extreme measures, to see what it can develop into. He thinks of how the book has to start, where in the plot he wants it to end, and then fills in the middle. Plot twists and unexpected turns are what he enjoys and leaves things open to his readers to think about for themselves, rather than be too specific on descriptions. His motto for writing is:

"Do not shy away from being open about something. Write what you would expect to happen, not what someone else wants. You are writing the book, not someone else."

Darius writes while listening to a mixed bag of music, from Mozart and Beethoven, to Queen and Led Zeppelin, letting the ideas flow with ease. His imagination is all over the place, and he prefers to be at his books for a long time. His ideas are sometimes bounced around among friends, just to get a different perspective, and see how much of that can be incorporated into the story.

RECAP OF NAMES AND LOCATIONS

NAMES of the chosen ones:

Ake: A fourteen-year-old boy, from Logder. Favoured weapon is double-bladed axe. Standing in at 6'3" and 82 kgs, the Grey Wolf, Hadver watches over him. Power is super hearing.

Anne: A fourteen-year-old girl, from Leonis. Favoured weapon is her mind, which is sharper than the others'. Standing in at 6'2" and 75 kgs, the Claw Lion, David watches over her. Power is brute strength.

Chris: A sixteen-year-old boy, from Covis. Favoured weapon is solid metal mace. Standing in at 6'0" and 70 kgs, the Mountain Raven, Cronder watches over him. Power is changing body structures.

Clint: A seventeen-year-old boy, from Covis. Favoured weapon is trident-cum-spear. Standing in at 6'5" and 80 kgs, the Black Raven, Cyrus watches over him. Power is that he can assess any threat and find a solution to fight it.

Dan: A fifteen-year-old boy, from Equis. Favoured weapon is bow and arrow. Standing in at 6'0" and 76 kgs, the Blue Roan, Frea watches over him. Power is that he can sense the emotions of animals and humans.

Edward: A seventeen-year-old boy, from Talis. Favoured weapon is flames that he can produce and use to fly, among other things. Standing in at 6'4" and 76 kgs, the Fire Dragon, Ontemp watches over him. Power is that he doesn't crack under pressure.

Elesa: A fourteen-year-old girl, from Logder. Favoured weapon is sword. Standing in at 6'2" and 85 kgs, the Grey Wolf, Ketta watches over her. Power is uncontrolled rage that supplies great amounts of strength.

Emmanuel: A seventeen-year-old boy, from Tauris. Favoured weapon is club of mountain birch. Standing in at 6'6" and 78 kgs, the Hump Bull, Aral watches over him. Power is that he doesn't back down from a fight, even if he knows that he will die.

Garon: A fifteen-year-old boy, from Logder. Favoured weapon is dagger. Standing in at 6'5" and 84 kgs, the Ag Wolf, Edmund watches over him. Power is super sight, for any environment.

Gonth: A fifteen-year-old boy, from Tauris. Favoured weapon is sword and shield. Standing in at 6'2" and 81 kgs, the Poison Bull, George watches over him. Power is that he can see the result of any battle beforehand, with whatever information he is given.

Isabella: A fifteen-year-old girl, from Equis. Favoured weapon is traps made by her. Standing in at 6"0" and 86 kgs, the Blue Roan, Esquire watches over her. Power is her ability to sense traps or ambushes from a distance.

Jacob: A sixteen-year-old boy, from Leonis. Favoured weapon is knuckledusters. Standing in at 6'1" and 83 kgs, the Cut Lion, Zoh watches over him. His power resides in his ability to intimidate others.

James: A fourteen-year-old boy, from Covis. Favoured weapon is knives. Standing in at 6'3" and 82 kgs, the Mountain Raven, Riyo watches over him. Power is turning invisible.

Karen: A fourteen-year-old girl, from Tauris. Favoured weapon is scythe. Standing in at 6'4" and 70 kgs, the Poison Bull, Qezre watches over her. Power is being an expert at torture.

Robert: A fifteen-year-old boy, from Equis. Favoured weapon is hands, being a specialist in hand-to-hand combat. Standing in at 6'2" and 85 kgs, the Strawberry Roan, Darius watches over him. Power is being able to hide his emotions from others.

Trest: A fifteen-year-old girl, from Talis. Favoured weapon is a customised scalpel. Standing in at 6'0" and 70 kgs, the Fire Dragon, Dersyu watches over her. Power is quick healing, and can heal others quickly as well.

Victoria: A sixteen-year-old girl, from Talis. Standing in at 6'1" and 80 kgs, the Sharp-Winged Dragon, Phiroze watches over her. Power is pheromonal manupilation.

Vincent: A sixteen-year-old boy, from Leonis. Favoured weapon is javelin. Standing in at 6'0" and 85 kgs, the Claw Lion, Nilesh watches over him. Power is accurate missile projection up to half a league.

NAMES of the district ring bearers:

Adrian: A fifteen-year-old boy, from Tauris.

Adriana: A sixteen-year-old girl, from Equis.

Hasha: A fourteen-year-old girl, from Logder.

Thomas: A fourteen-year-old boy, from Leonis.

Vesper: A fifteen-year-old girl, from Talis.

NAMES of the Gods:

Esdah: God of the Underworld.

Sorenth: God of War.

Ara: Goddess of Ice.

NAMES of the Antagonists:

Yedgal: The Dead Tyrant, killed by Rendaf's father.

Xristos: General of Yedgal's army.

Raze: Captain of Yedgal's private guard

NAMES of the districts, with some history:

Covis: The Raven District, founded by Lord Covin. Sacred gem is the Schrol. Ruled by Lord Nora, overseen by King Rendaf.

Equis: The Horse District, founded by Lord Equin. Sacred gem is the Rhodonite. Ruled by Lord Baki, overseen by King Rendaf.

Leonis: The Lion District, founded by Lord Leonin. Sacred gem is the Fire Opal. Ruled by Lord Xast, overseen by King Rendaf.

Logder: The Wolf District, founded by Lord Logder. Sacred gem is the Emerald. Ruled by Lord Huy, overseen by King Rendaf.

Talis: The Dragon District, founded by Lord Talin. Sacred gem is the Citrine. Ruled by Lord Veryu, overseen by King Rendaf.

Tauris: The Bull District, founded by Lord Taurin. Sacred gem is the Amethyst. Ruled by Lord Amlay, overseen by King Rendaf.

INKFEATHERS PUBLISHING

India's Most Author Friendly Publishing House

Stay updated about the latest books, anthologies, events, exclusive offers, contests, product giveaways and other things that we do to support authors.

 Inkfeathers Publishing

 @InkfeathersPublishing

 @_Inkfeathers

 @Inkfeathers

 Inkfeathers.com

We'd love to connect with you!